HONEYMOON WITH THE RANCHER

BY
DONNA ALWARD

MILLS
BOON

First published in Great Britain 2011
Harlequin Mills & Boon Limited,
Eton House, 18-24 Paradise Road, Richmond, Surrey TW9 1SR

© Donna Alward 2011

ISBN: 978 0 263 21976 0

Harlequin Mills & Boon policy is to use papers that are natural, renewable and recyclable products and made from wood grown in sustainable forests. The logging and manufacturing process conform to the legal environmental regulations of the country of origin.

Printed and bound in Great Britain
by CPI Antony Rowe, Chippenham, Wiltshire

A busy wife and mother of three (two daughters and the family dog), **Donna Alward** believes hers is the best job in the world: a combination of stay-at-home mum and romance novelist. An avid reader since childhood, Donna always made up her own stories. She completed her Arts Degree in English Literature in 1994, but it wasn't until 2001 that she penned her first full-length novel and found herself hooked on writing romance. In 2006 she sold her first manuscript, and now writes warm, emotional stories for the Harlequin Mills & Boon® Romance line.

In her new home office in Nova Scotia, Donna loves being back on the east coast of Canada after nearly twelve years in Alberta, where her career began, writing about cowboys and the west. Donna's debut Romance, HIRED BY THE COWBOY, was awarded the Booksellers Best Award in 2008 for Best Traditional Romance.

With the Atlantic Ocean only minutes from her doorstep, Donna has found a fresh take on life and promises even more great romances in the near future!

Donna loves to hear from readers. You can contact her through her website at www.donnaalward.com, visit her MySpace page at www.myspace.com/dalward, or through her publisher.

To Liz Fielding: inspiration, mentor, and friend.
Thank you, Liz, for just being you, and for
taking me under your wise and witty wing.

CHAPTER ONE

"¿SEÑORITA? We are here."

Sophia straightened in the seat and peered out the window at the vast plain, her eyebrows snapping together in confusion. Antoine had told her that *Vista del Cielo* translated into View of Heaven. She liked that idea. It conjured up images of wide blue skies dotted with puffy clouds, perhaps seen from a comfortable deck chair with a mimosa in hand. The sky was right, but looking out, Sophia saw nothing but waving grass and a dirt drive flanked by a row of trees. "This can't be it. There must be a mistake."

"No, *señorita.*" The driver's accent was thick. "*Esta* Vista del Cielo." He took his hand off the steering wheel and pointed at a small white sign at the end of the long drive.

A sickening, crawling feeling began in Sophia's stomach. The pampas spread out before her, flat and brownish-green. She slid across the back seat and looked out of the other side of the car. It was exactly the same view. On either side the fields spread, endless and dull. Off to her right, one huge gnarled tree looked out of place standing alone, a leafy green sentinel. And ahead, a house. A nice house, but definitely not a hotel. The building was large, a sprawling one story that turned two corners. A low roof over a stone patio added cozy atmosphere and contrasted with white stucco. Flowers in colourful pots stood here and there all along the front patio and another twisted tree formed a soft canopy over one side. It was beautiful, but clearly a family home, not the four or even five-star accommodations Antoine usually insisted upon when booking his travel.

The driver pulled to a stop in front of a shed and put the car into Park. "Don't leave," Sophia commanded. "This is a mistake." She fumbled for the Spanish words. *"Por error,"* she tried. *"No...vayas."* She knew the grammar was incorrect but hoped he'd catch her meaning. Perhaps she should have spent longer learning some important Spanish phrases. She flashed him a smile. She had to find out exactly where she was supposed to be and then get the cab driver to take her there.

"Si, señorita," he replied, and at last got out to open the door for her. This had to be wrong, all wrong. Where were the luxury rooms? The spa and gym? The dining area with a chef and wait staff?

For a moment her bravado failed her. She'd shored it up to make the trip alone, wanting—no, needing—to do this for herself. She'd wanted to find a way to stick it to Antoine for humiliating her so much. What could make a better statement than going on their honeymoon without him?

But that had all been based on things going smoothly and exactly to plan. She finally admitted to herself that she should actually have studied the plan a little more closely. She should have known the route. Especially traveling solo. What would she do now?

Then she remembered what had driven her to this point in her life and she steeled her spine. It had been wrong to accept Antoine's proposal in the first place and discovering his indiscretion had been a disaster. Still, if she had to be thankful for anything it was that she'd found out before the wedding and not after. She had given him three years of her best work, all the while falling for his kind words and sexy smiles. She'd thought herself the luckiest woman ever when he'd asked her out the first time. Marriage had seemed like the next logical step. Everyone had said it was meant to be, and she'd believed them.

But now she knew that Antoine had wanted nothing more than a trophy wife, the proper person on his arm to look good for the public. It wasn't enough for her. She hadn't realized until that moment—walking in on him making love to his mistress—that she wanted more. She didn't want the country club existence that was so important to her mother. She wanted more than appearances. She wanted respect, not betrayal. Love, not suitability.

Acceptance.

And in that defining moment, as her future had crumbled away, she'd found the courage to say no. And to walk away.

Which had led her here. Still, she was sure there had to be a mistake. She took a few steps forward, trying to make out the plaque on the front of the house. It was old and in Spanish, but she made out the words *Vista del Cielo* and the year—1935.

A roar and a cloud of dust had her swinging her head back towards the taxi, only to find the cabbie had dumped her luggage and was now driving back down the lane, tires churning up the dry earth like a dusty vapour trail.

"Wait!" She called after the taxi, running forward as fast as she could in her heels. But he didn't pause or even slow down. In moments he was gone, leaving her stranded with her bags in the middle of Nowhere, Argentina.

Her heart pounded. No one had come from the house to greet her. The place looked abandoned. She took a breath. Told herself to calm down. She would find a way out of this.

What she knew for sure was that she would not panic. She would not cry or indulge in hysterics. She reached for her purse and the cell phone inside, but paused. No. She most definitely would not make a phone call home for her mother to bail her out of trouble. She could handle this on her own.

Her mother had barely spoken to Sophia since she had cancelled the wedding. There was no question of asking Antoine, either. It would be a cold day in hell before she'd ask him for anything ever again.

She took a step forward, feeling the heel of one of her favourite Manolos sink into the soft earth. She gritted her teeth. Why was it that the first time in her life she did anything impulsive, it turned out like this? If it had happened to anyone else, she'd have had a good laugh at the comedy in the situation. But it wasn't happening to someone else, it was happening to her. And the truth was, behind the designer shoes and the skirt and the French manicure, she was scared to death.

She'd been running on righteous indignation for weeks now, and, if she let it, being alone in a strange country could be the straw that broke her back.

"Hola," a voice called out, and she turned her head towards the sound, her shoulders dropping with relief. At least someone was here who could explain the mix-up. Antoine had told her that they were staying at an estancia—a guest ranch—with all the amenities. It had sounded lovely and serene. But she knew Antoine. He never settled for anything except the best. She'd prepared for the trip based on that assumption, and now she wasn't prepared at all. Sometimes it felt as though everything she thought she knew had been turned upside down, and it was hard to find her feet again.

A man stepped out of the shadows by the barn door and Sophia swallowed.

Whatever she had expected to find here in the middle of nowhere, it wasn't this. The man approaching with long, lazy strides was perhaps the best looking male creature she'd ever clapped eyes on. He wore faded jeans and boots and a T-shirt that had seen better days. What was surprising was his face. He had a crown of thick, slightly wavy black hair and gorgeous brown eyes fringed with thick black lashes that most women would die for. The golden tone of the skin over his high cheekbones set his dark looks off to exotic perfection.

What was a man like that doing in a place like this?

"Hello," she called out, attempting to calm her suddenly increased heart rate. She shrugged it off, telling herself that just because she'd sworn off men she wasn't *dead*. She pasted on a smile, fighting to quell the anxiety swirling through her veins. "Perhaps you can help me." After the incident with the cabbie, she felt compelled to add, "Do you speak English? *¿Hablas inglés?*"

"Of course. What is the problem?" His black gaze looked at her suitcases, then her, and then slid down to her feet, to the peacock-blue pumps, one with a now very dirty heel. He raised an eyebrow as he examined the four-inch stilettos and a smile flirted with his lips before he looked back up. She schooled her features into a bland mask. She needed his help, and it didn't matter a bit if he approved of her shoes or not. They would have been perfectly appropriate for the upscale accommodation she'd expected.

"I'm afraid I've been delivered here in error, and the taxi driver didn't speak English. He simply dropped my bags and left. I was hoping you could help me sort this out?"

"Of course."

She smiled, feeling much better knowing she had an ally. "I was supposed to arrive at the Vista del Cielo this afternoon. He claimed this is it, but I am sure he was wrong."

"This is the Vista del Cielo, but you were not expected."

Her smile faltered as alarm jolted through her body. "Perhaps there is another Vista del Cielo?" she suggested, trying desperately to sound pleasant and not panicked. "I am booked there for the next week."

The man's scowl deepened. "No, we are the only one. But we have no bookings for this week. We did, but it was cancelled last month."

"This *is* a hotel, then."

"An estancia, yes. A guest ranch."

A guest ranch. This was no mistake, she realized with a sinking heart. She remembered Antoine's voice as he'd teased her. *It will be different,* he'd boasted. *Lots of privacy for a newly married couple.*

Looking back now, the idea made her blush. The thought of being here alone with Antoine made her suddenly self-conscious in front of the man before her. Thank goodness she'd at least been spared that.

Still, it seemed inconceivable that Antoine, with his lavish tastes, would have booked them here. It looked quiet and peaceful—a definite bonus to her—but it still didn't seem to compute with what she'd expected. "Where is the spa? The pool?" After her long dusty trip, the idea of dipping into the pool for a refreshing swim sounded heavenly. Perhaps a hot tub to soothe the muscles that had been cramped up in an airplane and then the taxi. She could nearly feel the bubbles on her skin already. Maybe this place was more rustic than she'd anticipated, but she knew Antoine would have demanded a certain standard.

"That's why we had to cancel the reservations. There was a fire. I'm afraid the spa building as well as others were destroyed. Thankfully the house was spared."

Everything in Sophia went cold and the polite smile slid from her face. "Fire?"

"Yes…we've cancelled everything until the repairs are made and things rebuilt. The pool made it through, but we've had to have it drained because of the ash and debris."

Sophia felt a growing sense of despair. She stared around her, wondering how things could have gone so perfectly pear-shaped. Her gaze caught on the odd looking tree, standing like a solitary sentinel in the middle of the plain. It looked exactly as she felt. Alone. And lonely. She was beginning to understand that they were two completely separate things.

"Perhaps if you told me your name, we could sort it out," he said, a little impatiently.

"The reservation was under Antoine Doucette."

The man's face changed as understanding dawned. "The honeymoon." Then he looked confused again, looked at her cases, and back again. "And the other half of the happy couple?"

Sophia lifted her chin. She could do this. She could. She could get past the embarrassment and the hurt and explain dispassionately. She had faced worse in the last months. She'd faced Antoine, her family and friends, even the chokehold of the press closing in around her. She could handle one annoying Argentinian...whatever he was. Farmer? Gaucho? Who was he to judge her?

"I came alone. I'm afraid the marriage did not take place."

"I see. I am sorry, *señorita*."

His words said apology but his tone certainly did not. It was strictly polite and almost...cold. "Don't be," she replied, putting her hand on her hip. "I'm not." It was only a half lie. She wasn't sorry she had called off the wedding. Under the circumstances it had been the right thing to do.

But it had been far from easy. She'd bear the scars from it for a long, long time.

A huff of surprise erupted from his mouth, followed by mutterings in Spanish that she couldn't understand. That made her angry. It made her feel inadequate and even more of an outsider, and she was tired of that feeling.

"Why were we not notified of the cancellation, then?" She pressed on, annoyed.

"I don't know." His brow furrowed. "Maria handles all the reservations and business. I can't imagine her making a mistake."

"Someone did. I'm here, aren't I?"

And so she was. She had to convince him to let her stay.

Antoine had thrown in her face how he'd not bought travel insurance and her breaking their engagement would cost him thousands of dollars. She'd told herself she had nothing to feel guilty about—after all, he was the one who'd been caught red-handed. She'd also spent money on a wedding that had never happened. The dress. The deposits for the printer, the reception, flowers, cake—all the trappings of a society wedding. His protests about the honeymoon money had fallen on deaf ears. It was only money. It would take a long time to replace it, but it would take longer to erase the pain of his betrayal. It was the betrayal that had hit her deep in her soul. She had been blind, had not recognized the signs. She had been left wondering if she could ever trust her own judgment again.

And now she was in Argentina with no place to stay.

She could go back to Buenos Aires. She could try to change her ticket and go home with her tail between her legs. Or she could book herself in somewhere and stay for the duration. It would mean taking most of her savings to pay for the hotel and food, but she'd have her dignity.

Wouldn't Antoine have a laugh about that? And she could already hear her mother chiding, *I told you it was a mistake to take that trip alone.*

That hurt. At a time when she'd most wanted her mother's support, it hadn't been there. Margaret Hollingsworth had thought she was crazy to call off the wedding and a life of security. Sometimes Sophia wondered why she kept trying to gain her mother's approval. Once, as a child, sad and missing her dad, she'd hidden in a cellar, not wanting her mother to see her tears. But she'd ended up locked in by accident, unable to get back out again. It had been hours before she'd been found, crying and terrified. Even now, she could still feel the dark, damp chill and hear her mother's furious words when what she'd wanted was a hug and reassurance. It was a hurt that had scarred her heart that day, and she'd never forgotten it.

But she couldn't spend her whole life seeking approval from

someone else. She knew that now. It was time for her to stand up for herself. To make her own happiness. She straightened her shoulders. She'd make the best of it and move forward.

"I insist on staying the week," she said clearly. "I did not receive notification that our booking was cancelled, and I have flown all the way from Ottawa. I have no intention of going back." She leveled a gaze at him, hoping that she appeared to mean business when inside she was trembling. He had to let her stay. The savings she had put aside were what she had been planning to use as a security deposit for a new, cheaper apartment, necessary now that she no longer had her well-paid job with Antoine. But there was pride at stake here and she relaxed her shoulders, determined to see it through.

The man's jaw hardened and his dark eyes glittered at her sharp command. "I am sorry, but we simply are not prepared for guests. I can arrange for you to go back to San Antonio de Areco. There is a hotel there. Or perhaps back to Buenos Aires."

Which sounded lovely, she supposed. Her gaze caught the strange tree again. It gave her a strong yet peaceful feeling. This place wouldn't be so bad. She would have time to relax and recharge. Besides, there was something in his dismissive tone that put her on edge. He was telling her what to do, and at some point she had to take charge of her own life. She'd been a people pleaser for years, always trying to do the right thing, not to create waves. This time it was up to her.

"But I want to stay here," she insisted firmly.

"No, you don't," he replied, calling her bluff. "I could see it on your face from the first moment. It is fine. Estancia life is not for everyone." He cast a disdainful look at her handbag and shoes. "Obviously."

Sophia gritted her teeth. He didn't think she could handle it? Obviously he hadn't ever been mobbed by the press at Parliament Hill or been surprised by a photographer shoving a camera in her face outside a downtown club and taunting her about political scandal.

"I insist," she replied. She looked around her at the plain surroundings. "Unless you can provide proof of the refund. In which case I am happy to pay the going rate if I am wrong."

Consternation showed on the man's face. She couldn't bring herself to back down an inch even though the prospect of spending her savings made her blanch. She was doing all she could just to keep it together. She wanted him to let her stay. Not just to prove something to Antoine, who probably couldn't care less. No, to prove something to herself. And most of all at this moment she wanted to be shown to her room, so she could close the door and decompress. Her legs suddenly felt weary—was it jet lag? And she had the oddest urge to cry. She was so tired. Tired of everything. Something had to give sooner or later and she really hoped that when it did, it would be in private. The past months seemed to catch up to her all at once, and she refused to cry in public.

The man stared at her for a moment, making her squirm inside. "I will try to get to the bottom of this. In the meantime, you'd better come in."

It wasn't exactly gracious, but Sophia felt weak with relief. Surely there was someone inside who could help her with her bags while this…man went back to work. If they were running an estancia, someone must be here to cook and clean and make sure the amenities were looked after. It didn't have to be fancy. A simple glass of wine and a hot meal would be most welcome.

Sophia held out her hand. "I'm Sophia Hollingsworth."

"Tomas Mendoza."

He took her hand in his and something twisted inside her, something delicious and unexpected. His hand was indeed firm, with slight calluses along the pads of his fingers. It was also warm and strong, and it enveloped her smaller, perfectly manicured one completely. It was a working man's hand, she realized. Honest. Capable.

"Miss Hollingsworth, I do not know if you realize what you're asking. Since we are shut down for another few weeks, the regular hosts of the estancia are away."

She waited, not exactly sure what he meant.

He pulled his hand away from hers. "Maria and Carlos Rodriguez normally run the place," he explained. "While I finish overseeing the repairs, they've gone to Córdoba to visit their son, Miguel. I will have to check the paperwork in the office for your reservation. At the same time, I need to make it clear that while they are away the full amenities are not available."

Dear Lord. So she was stuck here with a handyman? And who was to blame? Herself. Why hadn't she followed up before coming all this way? Another mistake to add to the list.

"And your job?"

He nodded at her. "I do what needs doing. I work with Carlos with the stock. Fix things. Do the trail rides."

Trail rides? Would he expect her to do that?

"One of our selling points is an authentic estancia experience. Our guests are encouraged to work alongside us."

She swallowed. If she backed out now she'd be giving in. Moreover, he'd know it. From deep inside came a need to rise to the challenge. But, for right now, the afternoon sun beat down on Sophia's head and she grew more tired by the moment. "Could you just show me to a room for now? I'm feeling quite hot. The air conditioning was broken in the taxi, and I'm really just trying to make sense of what's happened today."

"Certainly."

Tomas picked up two of her large cases, leaving the third, smaller carry-on, for Sophia. She put the strap over her shoulder and followed him along the gravel to the patio. He opened the front door and stepped inside, tugging her luggage in behind him.

For better or for worse, this was where she would be for the next week.

It could only get better from here, right? It would be what she made of it. She reminded herself of that fact as she followed Tomas down a hall and around a corner to her bedroom. His earlier polite smile had been replaced by a cool, emotionless expression. "You should be comfortable here," he said stiffly, opening the door to a room and then stepping back to let her pass. She stepped inside and instantly felt the stress of the last few months drain away.

"It's beautiful, thank you." It was simple and certainly no luxury suite. But it was brilliantly clean, meticulously cared for and suited her perfectly. The walls were pristine white, looking as though they'd been newly painted, and she immediately went to the open window that looked out over the grassy plain, stretching endlessly to the south. The air was clean, free of pollution and smog, and it refreshed her. More than that, the place was private, and privacy was something she craved quite desperately.

The bed was gorgeous, an intricately patterned iron bedstead adorned with linens the soothing colour of a summer sky. A basket of towels and toiletries sat on a low dresser, the plush cotton the same blue as the bedspread. Right now all she wanted was to sink into the bed's softness and let the stress of the day drain away.

She turned back to Tomas, suddenly aware that they were standing in what was now her bedroom. The silence stretched out awkwardly. There was nothing inappropriate about being in here with him. He was filling the role of concierge and apparently so much more. So why did she suddenly feel so self-conscious?

"What a lovely room."

"I am pleased you like it." The hard gleam in his eyes softened just a bit, as if her approval validated her in some way. As soon as she glimpsed it, the gleam disappeared.

What would it take to win him over? It was going to be a very long week if this was the extent of their conversation.

"It's so peaceful. Listen." She went to the window again, trying to escape his keen gaze. She pushed aside the curtain with a hand, looking out, leaning her head back so that the warm breeze caressed her throat. "Do you hear that?"

He came closer behind her, so close she could feel his presence by her shoulder even though he had to be several inches away. "Hear what?"

She laughed then, a carefree, feel-good laugh that she felt clear to her toes. The sound was unfamiliar to her ears, but very, very welcome. Suddenly the situation didn't seem so catastrophic. She had no one to please but herself this week. "That's just it. Nothing. I hear nothing, and it's wonderful." She closed her eyes and let the sunshine and wind bathe her face.

When she turned back around, the severe look on his face had disappeared. He understood, she realized. That took away the self-conscious part of being alone with him but left in its wake the flicker of attraction she'd felt when holding his hand. A flicker she wasn't sure what to do with.

She needed to escape his gaze and the nearness of him, so she moved to the dresser to touch the towels and trail her fingers over the wood. It was slightly scarred and Sophia loved how the markings added character to the piece. This was no sterile hotel room without a wrinkle or scratch. It wasn't about perfection. It had a level of familiarity and comfort that simply said *home*. The kind of home she'd secretly always wished for and had never had.

"That's the idea," he replied. "The city has its charms. But sometimes a person needs to get away to where things are…" he broke off the sentence, and Sophia wondered what he had been going to say. The impression she got was that big problems became small ones here. She found herself curious about him. Who was Tomas Mendoza? Why did this simple life hold such allure to him?

"Less complicated?"

Tomas stared out of the window as the moment drew on. "Yes, less complicated," he confirmed, but Sophia didn't feel reassured. Had his life been complicated once? For all his good looks, there was a wall around him, as though no matter what, he would keep people at arms' length. He was impossible to read.

"Just leave the bags," Sophia suggested. "I think I would like to freshen up and have a nap."

Sophia shouldered her tote bag and was just reaching for one of her suitcases when the tote slipped off her shoulder, catching on her elbow and knocking her off balance. Her heel caught as her right toe snubbed the edge of her biggest case and she lurched forward.

Straight into Tomas's arms.

He caught her effortlessly, his strong arms cinched around her as he righted her on her feet. Without thinking, she looked up. It was a mistake. Her cheeks flamed as she realized his hand was pressed firmly against her lower back. It was tempting, having her body pressed close to his, but the real trouble was the way their gazes clashed. She had not been held in such an intimate embrace for a long time, and never with the nerve-tingling effect she was suffering now. A muscle in Tomas's jaw tightened and Sophia's breathing was so shallow her chest cramped. For a breath of a moment she wondered what it would be like to be kissed by him. Really, truly kissed.

And behind that thought came the intimate realization that for the next several days, it was just the two of them here.

The thought tempted but also made her draw back. There was making a statement of independence by taking this trip alone, and then there was just being foolish. This was not why she had come. A holiday fling was not what she was looking for. She pushed away and out of his arms and straightened her blouse.

"In addition to poor fact checking, I think we can safely add klutz to my list of faults today," she joked, but the quip fell flat as she saw the wrinkle between his brows form once more.

"I hope not," he answered, pushing her suitcase into place at the end of the bed and straightening into that damnable rigid posture once more. "This is a working ranch, Miss Hollingsworth." He'd reverted to her formal English name again, backing away. "The Vista del Cielo was established to give guests an authentic gaucho experience. Our guests live like the locals for the duration of their stay. In the absence of our other facilities, I do hope you take advantage of all the estancia has to offer." Once again he looked at her shoes, then up at her tidy skirt and linen blouse, which was now wrinkled beyond recognition. "I hope you've brought other more... appropriate clothing."

Sophia felt like an idiot. She'd been so sure and so blindly determined to soak up every entitled minute that she'd thrown her best things in her luggage and jetted off. Now this gaucho was issuing a challenge. She hated the indulgent way he looked at her clothes. She'd show him. She'd do everything on his damned list of activities!

She sniffed. It wasn't as if she made a habit of falling down all the time, or worse, falling into men. She wasn't incapable. But he had hit on yet another obstacle—her suitcases were packed with totally inappropriate clothing. Bathing suits for lounging around a pool, a selection of skirts and dresses, all with matching shoes for Michelin-starred dinners with a view.

This wasn't Tomas's fault. It was hers, for not being more thorough. If she'd known what sort of establishment this was, she would have packed the proper things. Sometimes she felt as if she could do nothing right. She trusted in all the wrong things instead of relying on herself.

If she were determined to change, why not start now? She could fake it until she made it, right? She would show this Tomas that she could take on anything he dished out.

"I'm looking forward to it," she replied, desperate to save face. Did helping out also mean horseback-riding? She felt herself go pale at the thought. She'd ridden a horse exactly twice in her life. The first time the mare had been led by her halter. The second time had been a few years later when a friend at school had asked her to an afternoon at a local stables where she took lessons. That time Sophia had held the reins. She'd managed a very choppy trot but had nearly panicked when the horse had broken into a canter. She thought she was probably twelve when that had happened.

But she wasn't twelve any longer. She could handle herself better this time. She didn't want to look like a fool in front of him. Not when he looked so very perfect.

"First I think I would like to rest," she suggested, putting reality off a little while longer. When the time came, she'd go with him and she'd do just fine. "It has been a long flight and drive."

"Very well. While you are resting, I'll see what I can find out about this mistaken reservation."

His insistence that she was wrong grated. "Mr. Mendoza…"

He paused by the door and looked back at her. "Yes?"

She gave him her sweetest smile. "I appreciate you accommodating me during an inconvenient time for you. I do apologize for the disruption."

She tried a smile, an olive branch to smooth the way for the next few days. She knew that aggravating one's host—

especially a host who was already less than cordial—wasn't the way to get the best service.

"Dinner is at seven," he replied, unsmiling, and shut the door behind him.

In a fit of juvenile satisfaction, Sophia stuck her tongue out at the door before collapsing on the bed.

CHAPTER TWO

TOMAS had planned on a quick meal for one tonight but instead found himself making *locro*—a stew of beans, meat, corn and pumpkin. It was simple enough to make and something typically Argentinian for his guest.

Guest. He snorted, stirring the stew. What a mix-up. The first thing he'd done was check the books, but no notation had been made next to the name *Antoine Doucette*. Then he'd called Miguel's number in Córdoba. Maria remembered the reservation, but couldn't remember if she'd cancelled it. Tomas hadn't pushed; Maria was still traumatized by the fire. When Miguel had suggested they visit, Tomas and Carlos had agreed it would be good for Maria to get away for a few days. Tomas wanted her to see things nearly as good as new when she came back. The spa building had to be reconstructed, but the other outbuildings were nearly repaired. If things went well, they could even have the pool refilled and working in another week.

But it was Maria's words to him today that had caused him the most trouble. He'd explained the situation and Maria had instantly been sympathetic to Sophia's plight. "Take care of that girl, Tomas," she said firmly. Then she'd laughed. "She must be a real firecracker to take her honeymoon alone. She's your responsibility now. You will see to things until we return."

As if he needed reminding. He chopped into the pumpkin, scowling. Maria had been mothering him for so long that she sometimes forgot he was a grown man. He knew what his responsibilities were. They were impossible to forget.

"We'll sort the rest out when Carlos and I come back. Maybe we'll come Wednesday now."

"There's no need..."

But Maria had laughed. "She will be tired of your cooking by then. Wednesday. Just be nice, Tomas."

"I would never..."

"Yes, you would." Maria had laughed, but he knew she meant it. Maria and her family knew Tomas better than anyone else on earth. Too well.

Wednesday. That meant he had three days after today in which he not only had to do his work, but had to entertain Sophia as well. She'd put on a brave face, but he knew she had been expecting something totally different from what she was getting. He indulged in a half smile, but then remembered the look on her face when she'd thought he was going to send her away. She had been afraid behind all the lipstick and talk. And he had been just stupid enough to see it and go soft.

He turned down the heat and put the cover on to let the *locro* simmer. Going soft wasn't an option for him right now. The estancia wasn't due to reopen for another few weeks. There was still work to do—and lots of it. The boutique had to be restocked now that it was painted. The horses and the small beef herd Carlos raised still needed to be cared for. The storage shed behind the barn had been rebuilt since the fire, but the paint for the exterior was sitting in the barn, waiting for Tomas to have a few spare moments. As if. And the builders had had another job lined up, which was why it was taking longer for the pool house to be rebuilt.

With Carlos here, they could have muddled through just fine. But they'd agreed that getting Maria away for a few days—letting her visit her son—was a better course of action.

Tomas simply hadn't counted on babysitting a spoiled princess and playing cook and maid. That was normally Maria's area of expertise, and he and Carlos stuck to the outdoors. The estancia was a business that ran smoothly, just the way they'd planned, with everyone playing to their strengths. He could stay in the background, exactly where he liked it. He was polite and friendly to guests. They were only strangers passing through, asking nothing more from him than a trail ride and some local history. They made the same mistake Sophia had made today—assuming he was the jack-of-all-trades around the place. That was fine, too. He stayed a silent partner in Vista del Cielo and got the peace and isolation he craved. Carlos and Maria had their livelihood. Everyone was taken care of.

He heard a noise from down the hall and guessed that the princess was waking from her slumbers. He imagined briefly what she would look like asleep on the blue coverlet, her hair spread out in a great auburn curtain around her. He shook his head and reached for a pair of bowls from the cupboard. There was no denying she was beautiful. Stunning, actually, with her dark red curls and roses-and-cream complexion. Maybe she had a sense of entitlement about her and was used to getting her own way, but he could see why. She'd turned her dark eyes on him and said she was tired and he'd left her to nap without a word. Now he was finishing dinner and setting the table when the whole purpose of this place was for everyone to work together. It was one of their biggest selling points. A feeling of family.

And that was something he had no desire to feel with Sophia Hollingsworth.

"Something smells delicious."

He nearly dropped the bowls when she appeared in the doorway behind him.

Her hair was down but slightly tousled from sleep, the curls falling softly over one shoulder. Heavy lidded eyes blinked at him and she was several inches shorter, thanks to the fact that she'd left her shoes in her room and appeared in bare feet. That was why he hadn't heard her approach. His gaze stuck on ten perfectly painted coral toenails. She had extraordinarily pretty feet, and even without the shoes he could tell she had a great set of legs hiding beneath her straight skirt.

It was the princess, unwrapped, and he swallowed, realizing he found her very appealing indeed. At least physically.

That was the last thing he needed.

"Did you sleep well?" He turned away from her, putting the bowls on the table.

"Yes, thank you. I feel very refreshed."

Her voice was soft and Tomas felt it sneak into him, down low.

"I didn't mean to sleep so late," she apologized, and he swallowed as the husky tone teased his ears. "Whatever you've cooked smells wonderful."

"It's nothing fancy." He turned back to her and steeled his features. He would not be swayed by a pretty face and a soft voice. Damn Carlos and Maria. If they were here, they could handle Miss Princess and he would be in the barn where he liked it. "I do not usually do the cooking."

"I'm not used to a man cooking for me at all, so that in itself is a treat." She blessed him with a shy smile.

His pulse leapt and he scowled. His physical response to her was aggravating. "I expect you're more accustomed to five-course meals and staff to wait upon you, right?"

A look of hurt flashed across her face and he felt guilty for being snide. He was just about to apologize when the look disappeared and she furrowed her brow. "What makes you say that?"

"Oh, *querida*." The apology he'd toyed with died on his lips and he reached into a drawer for cutlery. "You practically scream high maintenance. It is clear you are used to the best. Which makes your presence here alone all the more intriguing."

"High maintenance?" A pretty blush infused her cheeks. She really was good, he thought. An intriguing combination of innocent ingénue and diva. Maybe a few days mucking around a ranch would be good for her. It had certainly done wonders for him.

She stepped forward, the soft, injured look gone. "I see," she said. "You think I'm some sort of pampered creature who lives to be waited upon."

"Aren't you?"

"Not even close."

"Oh, come on." He finished setting the table and turned to face her. "Designer clothes, perfect hair… You expected to arrive at some retreat or spa, didn't you? Not a working estancia. Admit it."

Her cheeks blazed now, not with embarrassment but with temper. "Okay, fine. Yes, this is not what I expected. You are not what I expected."

He smiled with satisfaction. "No, I am not. If you're not up to it, say so now. I'll arrange for you to return to Buenos Aires tomorrow." There, he decided, he'd given her a perfectly legitimate out. The few hours it would take to drive her back to the city would be worth it to have the rest of the week free to work. Better yet, she'd be gone before Maria and Carlos got back. Maria would get ideas into her head. She'd been prodding lately about Tomas getting away more. That he needed to stop hiding. That he should find a nice girl.

Not that a woman like Sophia, on her solo honeymoon would qualify in Maria's eyes, but it would be better all around if the potential were erased altogether. Tomas didn't want a nice girl. He didn't want to get away more. He wanted the life he'd chosen here on the pampas. Simple and uncomplicated. He'd chosen it to help him forget.

His insides twisted. Some days now he tried to remember. Forgetting seemed so very wrong. Disloyal.

"And you'd like that, wouldn't you."

Her saucy tone turned his head. *"¿Perdón?"*

"Are you trying to get rid of me, Mr. Mendoza? Get me out from under your feet? This wasn't my mix-up. You think by threatening me with some honest work I'll run and hide away somewhere where staff will wait on me hand and foot?"

"Isn't that what you want?"

She paused for a moment, then leveled him with a definitive glare. "No."

"No?" He raised an eyebrow.

"No. I want to stay."

"I checked the books and spoke to Maria, by the way."

"And?"

"And the refund isn't notated in the regular spot and Maria doesn't remember. She said she will straighten everything out when she comes back on Wednesday."

"And then Wednesday you will see," Sophia replied confidently.

"You realize what I'm saying, right? People who stay at the estancia participate in all kinds of activities. Working with the animals, in the barns. Even in the house. They become one of the family. With the hard work and the benefits, too."

"You don't think I can do it?"

He looked at her, all hairdo and perfect makeup and pedicured feet. "No, I don't."

"Then perhaps we're in for a week of surprises." She flashed him a superior smile. "Maybe now you can surprise me with what's cooking in that pot. I'm starving."

He'd expected her to heave a sigh of relief and take him up on his offer, not challenge him. He wasn't sure whether he admired her spunk or was frustrated by it.

But time would tell. Let her enjoy her home-cooked meal and scented bath tonight. Tomorrow would be a different story.

What to wear was definitely a quandary.

Sophia went through the open suitcase one more time, looking for something suitable. Clothing lay scattered on the bed like seaweed on a sea of blue linen. She checked her watch. Tomas had said breakfast at seven sharp, and it was already quarter past. Being late gave him even more ammunition. There had to be something here she could wear!

She held up a pair of trousers the shade of dark caramel and frowned. The only shoes she had that would match were the Jimmy Choo sandals she'd bought on sale during her last trip across the border. Why hadn't she thought to bring something more casual? A pair of sneakers. Yoga pants. But no, the only exercise wardrobe she'd packed was her swimsuits, thinking she'd be spending time beside the pool. Perhaps relaxing in a sauna. She looked in despair at the flotsam of clothes on the bedspread. How could she have been so stupid?

Seven twenty-five. She was so late. She remembered the way Tomas had looked at her last night and felt anger flow through her veins as she sifted through her suitcase again. He'd been patronizing. Granted, she hadn't made the best impression, and yes, she'd been shocked. She grabbed a sundress out of her second open case and pulled it over her head, out of time for further deliberation. For the last three years she'd been treated that way. She hadn't realized it then, but looking back now it was so very clear. She'd been more of a decoration than someone useful. That kind of treatment stopped today. It stopped with Tomas Mendoza and his superior attitude. If it took eating a little humble pie for breakfast, she'd do it.

She hurried down the hall to the kitchen. The smell in the room was to die for. A covered basket sat on the table and she lifted the towel. The rolls were still warm, soft and fragrant. Bread? He'd made bread?

She paused, her hand on the plate left at the place where she'd sat last night. She tried to picture Antoine making bread in the morning. The very idea was preposterous. He wouldn't even have made pastry out of one of those cans in the refrigerated section of the grocery store. Heck, Sophia had never made bread from scratch in her life.

The breakfast was completed with a bowl of fresh fruit and coffee waiting in the pot, hot and rich.

She'd missed mealtime, and the thought stole the smile from her face. She'd have to eat quickly and then find Tomas. Showing up late was not the way to get off on the right foot. Hurriedly she buttered a roll and poured a half cup of coffee. When she was done she put her plate in the sink and the platter of fruit back in the fridge. She went outside, feeling the warmth of the morning soak into her skin as she searched for Tomas. She nearly ran into him turning a corner towards the outbuildings at the back.

"Oh!" she gasped, stopping short and nearly staggering backwards. She would have if he hadn't steadied her with a quick hand on her arm. His warm grip sent a shaft of pure pleasure down to her fingertips. He let her go as soon as she was stable and dropped his hand.

"I see you're up."

"Yes, I'm sorry I'm late. I slept so well…" She would sweeten him up. She would let him know his garrulousness didn't get to her. "My bed is very comfortable."

"Apparently."

The pleasure went out of Sophia like air from a balloon. But she wouldn't give up yet. She'd kill him with kindness if that's what it took. "The rolls were still warm. Did you make them?"

He stood back, looking at her as if he were measuring and finding her wanting. "Yes, I did. Maria showed me how long ago. When she returns you'll have real cooking, not my second-rate impression of it."

"I wouldn't call your cooking second-rate. The stew last night was delicious."

"I'm glad you liked it."

The politeness was a cold veneer, meaning little when she felt it wasn't sincere.

"So what did I miss?"

"Today's activity," he remarked dryly, and swept out an arm.

Behind them was a utility shed. Beside it were supplies for painting—a large bucket of paint, two smaller cans and brushes.

"Painting?" This was a vacation. Shouldn't there be guided tours? Even without the pool and other amenities, shed painting was hardly a unique Argentinian experience.

He shrugged. "You did say you were prepared to surprise me. So here we are. It needs to be done."

He was trying to get the best of her. She was sure of it. He was planning on pushing her until she quit. But she would not be dismissed. She smiled, quite enjoying the liberating feeling of making up her own mind. If Tomas said paint, she'd paint.

Just not in a sundress and heels.

"I'll need a change of clothes. I'm afraid I came unprepared for painting."

He shrugged again and headed towards the paint supplies.

"Señor Mendoza!"

To her credit, she did a brilliant job of rolling out the ñ in señor. He turned around, surprise flattening his face. She reveled in that expression for a fleeting second before continuing. "If you will please find me something to wear, it would be greatly appreciated."

"Do I look like a clothing store, Miss Hollingsworth?"

He put the emphasis on the *miss* just as she had with *señor* and it had her eyebrows lifting in challenge.

"There were brochures in my room." Oh, if she'd only thought to look at them at home before packing! Seeing them last night had made her cheeks flush with embarrassment, but there was nothing to be done about it now. "I know you have a boutique on site. Perhaps I might find something there?"

He scowled and she felt victory within her grasp.

"If you have any trousers at all, put them on. And meet me back here in five minutes." With a put-upon sigh, he disappeared.

She had gotten the better of him, and while it was a small victory, it felt good. He had to know she was not a meek little sheep that needed caring for. She was discovering she had a daring, adventurous side she'd never known existed. Oh, perhaps painting a shed wasn't very adventurous. But after being the girl who'd done as she was told, too afraid to do otherwise, all this felt absolutely liberating.

She skipped to the house and came back moments later wearing the caramel trousers and a white linen blouse. It was as casual as she had in her cases, but she'd remedy that somehow. Tomas came back holding a navy bundle in his hands and she drew her eyebrows together, puzzled. It didn't look like something from a boutique.

"Put these over your clothes," he said, handing her a pair of paint-splattered coveralls.

"You're kidding."

"You don't want paint on those clothes, do you?"

"No, but…"

"Anything from the boutique is brand new—you don't want paint on those things, either, do you?"

Why did he have to be right?

She put on the coveralls, hating the baggy fit but zipping them up anyway. The sleeves were too long and she rolled them up. And felt ridiculous standing there in her sandals.

She caught a glimpse of a smile flirting with the corners of his mouth. "Sure, go ahead, laugh. I know I look silly."

"Put these on," he said, handing her a pair of shoes.

"What are these?"

"Alpargatas."

She put on the canvas and rope shoes that looked like slip-on sneakers. They were surprisingly comfortable.

"I believe I am ready."

"I hope so. The morning is moving along."

Like she needed another reminder that she was late.

She followed him to the shed, admiring the rear view despite herself. Today he was wearing faded brown cotton pants and a red T-shirt that showed off the golden hue of his skin, not to mention the breadth of his back and shoulders. He was unapologetically physical and she found herself responding as any woman would—with admiration. Seeing how capable he was made her want to succeed, too, even if it was just at the most menial task.

"Don't you have horses to feed or something?"

He shook his head. "I did most of the chores while the bread was rising."

"You didn't need to make bread on my account." She pictured his hands kneading the dough and wet her lips. He really was a jack-of-all-trades. It wasn't fair that he was so capable and, well, *gorgeous*. A total package. It made her feel very plain and not very accomplished at all.

"I was up. In Maria's absence, it is up to me to make sure you're looked after."

Great. He didn't need to say the words *obligation* and *burden* for her to hear them loud and clear.

"Is there nothing you can't do?"

"When the gaucho is out on the pampas, he is completely self-sufficient. Food, shelter, care of his animals…he does it all."

"And have you always been so capable?"

A strange look passed over his features, but then he cleared his expression and smiled. The warmth didn't quite meet his eyes. "Oh, not at all. It was Carlos who taught me. And I'll be forever in his debt."

Sophia wanted to ask him what that meant, but he reached down and grabbed a stick to stir the paint.

"Tomas?"

"Hmm?" He didn't look up from his paint. He kept stirring while Sophia's heart hammered. Getting the best of Tomas was one thing. But dealing with this relentless…stoicism was another. There was no sound here. Nothing familiar. All that she might have was conversation. It was the only thing to connect her to anything. And the only person she could connect to was Tomas.

"Could we call a truce?"

His hand stilled and he looked up.

"I know this is not what either of us planned. Can't we make the best of it rather than butting heads?"

His gaze clung to hers and in it she saw the glimmerings of respect and acceptance and something that looked like regret. That made no sense. But it was all there just the same.

"I am not generally very good company."

Sophia laughed a little. "Shocker."

Even Tomas had to grin at that. She saw the turn of his lips as he bent to his work again.

He handed her a can and a brush. "I thought you could start on the trim. You probably have a steadier hand than I do."

The shed wasn't big, but it did have two doors that opened out and a window on each of the north and south sides. Sophia held the can in her hand and wondered where to start. The door and windows had been taped to protect against errant brush strokes. She stuck the brush into the can and drew it out, heavy with the white paint.

"You've never painted before, have you?"

She shook her head.

Tomas sighed. Not a big sigh, but she heard it just the same and felt a flicker of impatience both at him and at herself for not being more capable. "It was never…" She didn't know how to explain her upbringing. Or her mother's philosophy on what was done and what wasn't. You hired people to do things like painting and repairs. They were the help. It had been made especially clear after Sophia's father had moved out. It was then that Sophia's mother had put her foot on the first rung of the social climbing ladder.

"We weren't much for do-it-yourselfing," was all she could bring herself to say.

He came over and put his hand on top of hers. "You've got too much paint on the brush. It will just glop and run. This way."

Sophia bit down on her lip. His hand was strong and sure over hers, his body close. Her shoulder was near his chest as he guided her hand, wiping excess paint off the bristles. "There. Now, if you angle your brush this way…" He showed her how to lay the brush so the paint went on smoothly and evenly. "See?"

"Mmm hmm." She couldn't bring herself to say more. She was reacting to his nearness like a schoolgirl. His body formed a hard, immovable wall behind her and she wondered for a moment what it would be like to be held within the circle of his arms.

She pulled away from his hand and applied the paint to the trim, chiding herself for being silly. The purpose of the trip was to do something for herself, to show her independence. It was not to get besotted over some grouchy gaucho.

Tomas cleared his throat and went back to pick up his own brush.

As they put their efforts into painting the shed, Sophia stole a few moments to look around. The morning was bright, the air clear and fresh. The area around the barn was neat and trimmed and beyond it she saw a half-dozen horses or so seeking shade at one end of a corral, their hides flat and gleaming. Birds flitted between bits of pampas grass, singing a jaunty tune.

No traffic. No horns honking or elbows pushing. Also no shops, no conveniences, no restaurants.

It was stunning, but it was very, very isolated.

"How long have you been at Vista del Cielo?

"Three years."

"You've worked for the Rodriguezes all that time?" She slid excess paint off her brush against the lip of the can, but looked around the corner when Tomas paused in answering.

"Pretty much."

Hmm. Having him answer questions about the estancia wasn't much easier than their previous conversations.

"It is quite beautiful here," she persisted. "You can see for miles. And the air is so clear."

"I'm glad it meets with your approval in some way," Tomas replied.

She defiantly re-wet her brush and worked on the trim of the window as Tomas moved to the main section around the corner. If this was a working ranch, then she'd work. Just like anyone else. Just because she'd never had to didn't mean she couldn't. She continued swiping the paint on the wood. What would Antoine say if he could see his very perfect fiancée now? The idea made her smile. She might hate the baggy coveralls, but knowing Antoine would drop his jaw at the sight of her gave her perverse satisfaction. And the work was surprisingly pleasant. Simple and rewarding.

"Is the morning meal something the female guests would do with Maria?" she asked, more determined than ever to get Tomas talking.

"Sure," he answered, filling his can once more with the white paint. "But not just the female guests. Everyone helps where they can. Before the fire, we had one guest who made cornbread every morning for a week. It melted in your mouth, even without butter. He said he got the recipe from his grand-mother. But his wife, she was hopeless in the kitchen. She was terrific at rounding up cattle, though. Once she got started."

Sophia grinned. "Well, well. A regular speech at last. I must make a note—cornbread makes Tomas talk."

He sent her what she supposed was a withering look, but there was little venom behind it this time, and she laughed.

"What are you good at, Sophia?" He efficiently turned the verbal tables.

She swallowed. The question took her by surprise. The lack of an answer was even more shocking. Was she really so lacking in self-assurance she couldn't recognize her own strengths? "I don't know."

"You don't know?"

Her pride was stung. She had worked as Antoine's assistant and had done a good job. She doubted Tomas would see it that way. "I'm good at answering phones and taking messages and keeping a schedule. I can type seventy-five words a minute."

Resentment bubbled up once more at how Antoine had used her capabilities for his own purposes, with complete disregard for any true feelings she might have. She stabbed the brush back into the can. "I'm good at showing up on time in the appropriate outfit, and saying the right things." She realized how empty and foolish that sounded. "I'm not good at much, it seems."

"Those things have their place," he said graciously, and she began to feel a bit better. "But not at an estancia."

The bubble burst. "I'm beginning to see that."

"Giving in?" he asked mildly.

She took out her brush and gave the window trim an extra swipe. "You wish. Maybe it's time I learned a new skill set. How'm I doing?"

It felt wonderful to let some of the old resentment go, to look forward. When she got back to Ottawa, she'd make some changes. She'd already resigned her job and this time she'd do something she enjoyed. Truth be told, she hated politics. She frowned, her brush strokes slowing. She thought about all the private meetings she'd set up, the hand shaking and air kissing. It was all so fake. There wasn't a man or woman among that crowd who wouldn't stab you in the back if it suited them. Then she thought of the wardrobe sitting in her suitcases. Yes, she loved those pretty things. They had made her feel feminine and, in her own way, important.

But maybe, just maybe, she'd sold her soul a bit to get them. Maybe Antoine hadn't been the only one to lie. Maybe she'd been lying to herself, too. Maybe she'd made up for the lack of the right things in her life by filling it up with *stuff*. Was she more like her mother than she thought? For years her mother had insisted Sophia participate in one thing or another, when all she had wanted was to curl up in her room with a good book. When had that shifted? When had status become so important to her, too?

How many other lies had she told herself?

She bit down on her lip and dipped her brush in the can. It was something to think about.

CHAPTER THREE

SHE was so lost in her ponderings that she didn't notice a long drip of paint trickling down the side of the building. "Watch what you're doing," Tomas called. "You'll want to swipe that drip."

It annoyed her to be under his supervision and she gritted her teeth, taking the brush and swiping it down the side of the shed. She was nearly to the bottom when a movement caught her eye. She jumped backwards, sending the paint can flying. At the clatter, Tomas came running around the corner while Sophia stared at the grass, shuddering. "Kill it! Kill it, Tomas!"

Tomas held his paint brush aloft as he stepped ahead to see what the trouble was. When he saw it, he scowled.

"It's a little wolf spider, that's all."

"Little?" she gasped. She shuddered and took another step back. Anything with a body bigger than a dime lost the right to be called "little" when it came to spiders, and this one was substantially larger than that. "You call that thing little?"

"It won't bite you. Even if it did, it wouldn't kill you."

Wouldn't kill her. There was a sense of relief knowing it wasn't poisonous, but Sophia's skin still crawled at the thought of the hairy eight-legged monster getting anywhere near her. She hated spiders. Hated them! The look of them. The thought of their legs on her skin. And the one at the base of the shed was the biggest she'd ever seen.

Tomas went forward and merely touched the spider with the end of his brush. The contact made it scuttle away to parts unknown. He picked up the paint can. Half the contents were on the grass, and wide white splashes went up the side of the shed, spatters on the glass of the window. He sighed, the sound impatient and aggravated.

He patiently took his brush and, with no concern for spiders whatsoever, moved it back and forth over the wall to blend in the spilled paint.

It made Sophia feel completely and utterly foolish. "I'm sorry," she murmured. "I have a thing about spiders." A huge thing. She knew she looked silly and the words to exonerate herself sat on her tongue. But she could not tell him why. It was too personal. Too hurtful.

"Maybe you'd like to work on the other side," he suggested. "I can finish here."

She would be a wreck trying to paint and watch for spiders at the same time. Maybe she looked like a diva, but even the thought of one crawling up her leg made her weak. Spiders and dark places were the two things she simply could not handle. "Will you check it for spiders first?"

He had to think her the most vapid female on the planet. But she could never tell him the real reason why she was afraid. The hours spent in the cellar had shaped her more than she could express. There'd been spiders there, too. Just small ones, but they'd crawled over her arms and she'd brushed them away, unable to see them. She'd held on to her tears that day until one had crept through her hair. It had completely undone her.

This was bad enough. She didn't need to let Tomas see any more of her faults.

Tomas accommodated her indulgence and checked the wall, foundation and grass surrounding the area. "Satisfied?"

"Yes, thank you." Sophia was embarrassed now. No wonder Tomas looked at her as though she was more trouble than she was worth. She dipped her brush and continued where Tomas had left off, determined to overcome the panic that still threaded through her veins. Not that she didn't watch. She did. Her eyes were peeled for any sign of foreign creatures. But if another spider came by, she would not scream or throw her paint can. She would shoo it away, just as Tomas had done.

The sun climbed higher in the sky and the air held a touch of humidity. Sweat formed on Sophia's brow as they worked on into the morning. She was beginning to appreciate all that went into a place like this. It wasn't just meals and fresh linen and saddling a horse or two. It was upkeep, making sure things were well-kept and neat. The plain shed was starting to look quite nice, matching all the other buildings with their fresh white paint, and there was a sense of pride in knowing it was partly to do with her efforts. There was pleasure to be found in the simplicity of the task. It was just painting, with no other purpose to serve, no ulterior motives or strategies. The sound of the bristles on the wood. The whisper of the breeze in the pampas grass, the mellow heat of the late summer sun.

She sneaked glances around the side of the building at Tomas. He had mentioned that Carlos had taught him the ways of the gaucho, but he had said nothing about himself, about where he came from. He could dress in work clothes but there was something about him, a bearing, perhaps, that made her think he wasn't from here. That perhaps he was better educated than he first appeared.

It was nearly noon when they finished the first coat, and Tomas poured what was left in their paint cans into the bucket, sealing the lid for another day and a second coat. "It's going to look good," he said, tapping the lid in place. He picked up the bucket and she watched the muscles in his arm flex as he carried it to the barn. She followed him, carrying the brushes, feeling indignation begin to burn. That was it? She'd worked her tail off all morning, and his only praise was *It's going to look good?* She sniffed. Perhaps what Tomas needed was a lesson in positive reinforcement. Or just being plain old nice!

She trailed behind him as they entered the barn. It was as neat as everything else on the estancia. The concrete floor was cool, the rooms and stalls sturdy and clean, the scents those of horses, fresh hay and aging wood. Tomas took the brushes from her and put them in a large sink. He started the water and began washing them out.

"You were a big help this morning."

Finally, some praise.

"Except when I threw paint everywhere."

"It is probably a good thing you didn't see him jump," Tomas commented.

She paled. "Jump?"

"*Si*. Wolf spiders—they don't really spin webs. They jump, and they're fast on the ground. Usually we don't come across them in the daytime. He scooted away, but when they jump…"

"Do we have to talk about this?"

"I find it very interesting."

He scrubbed at the brushes with a renewed energy. What he enjoyed was teasing her, she realized. There really was no need. She was already feeling quite foolish. She had no business being here. It was not her scene. The inside of her thumb was already blistered from holding the paint brush all morning.

Face it, Soph, she thought. *He was right. You're pampered and spoiled.*

She wished Tomas didn't see her flaws. The problem wasn't with the estancia or Tomas. It was her. She was the one lacking. She didn't want to be spoiled. What she wanted was validation. And somehow she wanted it from Tomas. She got the feeling that if she could earn *his* respect, she could earn just about anyone's.

Tomas finished with the brushes and laid them to dry. He was enjoying teasing her too much, and it unsettled him. It felt strange, like putting on old clothes that were the right size but somehow didn't fit just right anymore. He had left that teasing part of himself behind long ago. It disturbed him to realize it was harder and harder to remember those days. But seeing Sophia's huge eyes as he spoke of the spider, and then the adorable determined set she got to her chin when she was mad...

He should not be reacting this way. And it wasn't as if he was going to catch a break. Until Maria and Carlos came back, Sophia was his responsibility. Even his subconscious knew it. The bread making was not an attempt at being a good host. It was simply the result of waking far too early and needing to be busy to keep from thinking about her.

Which reminded him that it had been hours since they'd eaten.

"Come on," he said, leading the way out of the barn. "Let's get some lunch." Surely a meal was a good, safe activity. If he couldn't escape her, keeping occupied was the next best thing. And he was starving.

While Tomas got out the food, Sophia crawled out of the overalls and hung them on a peg. The meal was simple: a lettuce and tomato salad and cold empanadas that Tomas took out of the refrigerator. "Normally best when they are fresh and hot, but Maria made a batch before she left. It makes a quick lunch. I'll cook a proper dinner tonight."

He thought of the two of them sitting down to a meal together and frowned as an image of gazing at Sophia over candlelight flitted through his mind. It was too easy to stare at Sophia, admiring her heart-shaped face and the way her flame-tossed curls danced in the light. He hadn't missed the way her trousers cupped her backside, or that with her shirt button undone at her throat he could see the hollows of her collarbone. He wished for some interference to keep him distracted, but there would be none. And he would not let on that she got to him in any way, shape or form.

"Maybe I can help you. Cooking is one thing I can manage. Usually."

"Ah, so the princess has a skill."

He was baiting her again, but it was the easiest way to keep her at arm's length.

"Everyone has skills. Just because they're not like yours doesn't mean they don't exist."

She was right and he felt small for belittling her. What was getting into him? She was, he acknowledged. He'd been hiding behind his estancia duties for too long. With all the reconstruction after the fire, he was aware that things around the Vista del Cielo were changing. It wasn't the same place he remembered from when he'd first come here. Back then it had been simpler. Full of life and possibility. And Rosa. Her dancing eyes, her laugh had been in every corner. Now there were times he could barely recall her face; the memory seemed like a shadow of her real self, like a reflection in the water that could disappear with the drop of a pebble on the surface. Rosa was slipping further and further away, and damned if he didn't feel guilty about it.

And he was taking it out on Sophia.

"I'd appreciate the help," he offered as a conciliation.

As they sat down to the meal, Sophia looked at him curiously. "You're not from here, are you?"

Tomas looked up at her briefly, and then turned his attention to the platter of empanadas. "No."

"Where are you from, then? Where did you learn English? It's practically perfect. A hint of an accent, but otherwise..."

"Why do you need to know?"

Sophia huffed and toyed with her empanada. "I was just making conversation, Tomas. You do know what that is, right?"

Si, he'd been right. His social graces were so rusty they were almost nonexistent. Small talk. One didn't make small talk out here. But it had been part of his life once. He should remember how.

"I grew up in Buenos Aires, and went to private school in the U.S. for a few years. Then I came back and studied Engineering."

"Studying in the States?" Sophia's fingers dropped the pastry pocket as she gaped at him. "You have a degree in Engineering?"

He nodded, reminding himself to be very careful. He didn't like talking about himself, or the man he'd once been. Keeping it to plain old facts was plenty. "Yes, Mechanical Engineering. You're surprised."

"I am. How does a Mechanical Engineer end up working as a hired hand at an estancia?"

The explanation was long and unpleasant for the most part, and Tomas definitely wasn't sharing. It was better that she thought him simply the help. She'd look at him differently if she knew he was part owner of Vista del Cielo. And it would open up a lot more questions he had no desire to answer.

"This was where I wanted to be," he replied simply.

"It is quite a leap from engineering to the Vista del Cielo," she commented, biting into the pocket of spicy beef.

"Right."

Tomas went on eating, silent again. This hadn't always been his life. He'd let obligation and duty dictate until one day the price was too high. He'd let so many people down. His mother and father, who had such hopes for him and the family business. His brother, who was supposed to work by his side. And most of all, Rosa.

Carlos and Maria had offered him a place. He'd ended up making it his home. When he thought of his other life, it was like thinking about a stranger. Everything seemed so very far away.

"Tomas…"

"No, no," he said, pushing his plate away and leaning back in his chair. He forced a smile when he felt none, knowing that he had to change the subject. He ran his hand through his hair. "My turn. How does a pretty, pampered woman like yourself end up with a broken engagement? Who broke it off? You or him?"

As soon as he asked the question, he was surprised to find he wanted her to admit she'd been the one to call it off. It should have made no difference to him. He wasn't interested, so why did it matter if she was on the rebound or not? She hadn't sounded particularly sorry when she'd explained arriving alone yesterday, but then pain manifested itself in many ways.

"I did," she replied. She put down her last empanada and dusted off her fingers.

She looked so serious he felt compelled to tease her again, just to bring that light back to her eyes—even if it was anger. "What happened? Would he not keep you in the lifestyle to which you were accustomed?"

She raised her dark gaze to his, and he saw bleak acceptance. "Do you really think this is about lifestyle?" She smiled sadly. "If by lifestyle you mean affection and loyalty…" She looked down and cleared her throat before raising her head again. "Let's just say he was enjoying marital benefits— without the benefit of the marriage." She paused. "Or the wife."

Understanding dawned. The dog had gone elsewhere, all the while planning a wedding with Sophia. "He was cheating?"

"We never should have gotten engaged," she replied.

"Both of us were settling for what looked good, I suppose. I'm ashamed of that. I should have seen…"

He recognized self-blame when he saw it and for the first time he felt sorry for Sophia Hollingsworth.

But she surprised him by squaring her shoulders and pinning him with a direct, confident look. "At least I had the gumption to kick him to the curb when I found him with his…"

Tomas rattled off a few words in Spanish. The words were similar enough to English that Sophia puzzled them out and she burst out laughing. "Oh, thank you for that. That's perfect!"

Dios, she was beautiful, especially when she forgot herself and laughed like that. Her eyes lit up and her cheeks flushed rosy pink. How could her fiancé cheat on her? *Why* would he? She was a stunning, sensual woman, and he'd bet she had no clue of her own allure. He'd thought she was spoiled but now he was wondering if she'd just been sheltered. Either way, she hadn't deserved to be treated in such a fashion.

"For a man to do such a thing—he has no honour. Why would he stray? You're a beautiful woman."

Her gaze struck his, and he felt the impact clear to his toes. For a long moment a rich silence enveloped the kitchen as his gaze dropped to her full lips.

This was exactly what he needed to avoid. He cleared his throat, searching for words to break the spell. "A bit spoiled, perhaps, but not unkind, I don't think."

"Gee, thanks," she muttered, looking away. For a few seconds she studied her fingers and then she asked, without looking up, "You would never cheat on a woman, would you, Tomas?"

It was as if a cold breeze blew through the room and he froze. Cheat? No. But cheating was not the only way to wrong a woman. He'd failed Rosa in other ways. He rose from his chair and began gathering the dishes.

"Did I say something wrong?"

"It is nothing." He ran some water in the sink for dishes. This conversation had to end now. And he had to stop looking at her as if she were his favourite sweet. "This afternoon we need to ride. I will do these if you will go to the closet and find some boots that fit. And a hat. You may borrow one of Maria's, I think. The sun is already making itself known on your cheeks. You will also need some *bombachas*. They're in a box in the office. First door on your right."

"Some what?"

"*Bombachas*. Gaucho pants. You were right about the on-site boutique restocking—it is also on the agenda for this week."

"Where are we going?"

"I need to check the cattle this afternoon. We will ride out along the pasture. It is not a hard ride, Sophia. You will be fine."

Sophia looked down at her hands, torn between wanting to know about what had caused Tomas's abrupt change of subject and knowing she should probably let well enough alone. And that moment when she'd told him about Antoine…there had been something in his eyes that had taken her breath away. She wasn't used to a man having such a physical effect on her. There was a part of her that wondered if she could make it happen again, to feel that queer lifting in her chest when he settled his dark gaze upon her, or the shiver on her flesh the few times he'd touched her. She'd never felt anything quite like it before.

Not even with her fiancé. She looked down at her mani-cured nails, marred and slightly chipped from the morning's work. She was beginning to understand that the spa days and shopping sprees were only ways to cover what had been wrong from the start. Antoine had never loved her, and perhaps she'd never truly loved him, either. She'd only fancied herself in love.

It had hurt her incredibly that he'd taken a... No. She wouldn't even think the word *mistress*. It was too lofty a title for the tawdry piece he was...well, doing what ever he was doing on the side. She'd even blamed herself for a while, thinking that if Antoine had been satisfied at home he wouldn't have strayed. She had harsh memories of the things Antoine had said about her at the end. Like that she'd driven him to it. That she was an ice queen. Those words still hurt. Because on some level, she was afraid they were true.

But a man who loved her would have waited. He wouldn't have resorted to an affair. Tomas's words helped more than he could ever know. It hadn't been her fault. It had been Antoine's lack of character. And the way Tomas made her feel when he looked at her was anything but icy.

Sophia sat, nonplussed at the abrupt change as Tomas banged dishes around in the sink. Only moments ago they'd been talking about her and even laughing a little about her situation. And in a flash, the curtains were drawn again and Tomas was locked away.

She didn't feel it was the time to push. She stared at Tomas's back at the sink, so straight and rigid and unwelcoming. Perhaps he would relax during their ride. She guessed he was the type that would feel most at home out riding the pampas with the wind and wide open space for company.

Unlike her. Her heart quailed. She had known since arriving that she would end up on horseback. But she hadn't thought it would be today. For a second she considered confessing her inexperience to Tomas. But when she looked at him, his jaw was set in a tight line. He was shutting her out.

That was his right, after all. They were strangers, really, simply in the same place at the same time due to circumstance. He didn't owe her anything and she didn't owe him anything, either. And yet she was so tired of being shut out.

Of being in the background, patted on the head. She was sick and tired of her role as 'behaving appropriately' because she was too afraid to do anything else. Wear the right clothes, meet the right people, say the right things. And for whose benefit? Certainly not for hers. For her mother's ambition that Sophia would raise them above their station—and mostly for Antoine's political aspirations. He'd insisted that his success was hers as well, but she knew now that was a bunch of claptrap.

She wanted a success of her own. Even if meant riding a stupid horse across the pampas to impress a stubborn Argentinian. She wanted the disdain in his eyes to turn to admiration.

She found the box in the office and took out a pair of gray trousers, crestfallen at the pleating and narrow bottoms. They certainly weren't in vogue, but beggars couldn't be choosers. Then it was on to the closet for black boots and a hat with a rounded brim to shade her eyes. "If you'll excuse me for a moment, I'd like to freshen up. Put on some sunscreen before we go out."

"Take your time," Tomas replied. "I will have to saddle the horses anyway."

Sophia detected a note of satisfaction in his voice, as though he was pleased he'd diverted her questions. It only made her more curious and determined to find out what secrets he was hiding. He'd skilfully changed the subject, but she wanted to know what had led him to leave his life in the city for one of isolation in the pampas. A loner like the gaucho, relying on no one but himself.

She stood in the kitchen minutes later, feeling a bit conspicuous as she looked up at a framed picture on the wall. The woman in it was relaxed and happy, astride a black horse and beautiful in full gaucho gear. Sophia wondered what it would be like to be that comfortable in her own skin. And she wondered who it was. Maria, perhaps? Whoever, the picture made her feel somewhat foolish as she left the house and walked across the yard in her outfit. The boots were new and stiff and she felt ridiculous in the black hat that shaded her eyes, as though she was dressed up for Halloween. All she needed now was a poncho and a donkey, she thought.

And then she saw Tomas, waiting beside two horses. She blinked, looking at him with new eyes. He looked so different, so exotically handsome. He too had proper boots and a hat and a bandana tied around his neck. He looked the part of a romantic gaucho, while she felt like a complete imposter.

She inhaled and stepped forward. She could do this. It was simply a matter of faking it until it was true. She'd had lots of practice growing up.

"You look very authentic," he commented. So the ice man thawed a little, Sophia thought irritably.

"I feel sort of silly."

"Don't—you look the part. And you will appreciate the gear when you have been in the saddle beneath the sun." He smiled from beneath his hat. "Perhaps tomorrow if there's time, we can go into San Antonio de Areco and you can purchase a few things there to get you through the week. I don't expect your designer clothes will hold up well otherwise."

She knew he was right. She couldn't swan about in Chanel and Prada all week, and to be truthful the idea of a pair of plain old comfortable jeans was heavenly. How long had it been since she'd lounged around in comfortable clothes, enjoying the sunshine as she had this morning? The thought perked her up.

"Are you ready?"

She swallowed, remembering there was still the issue of her riding skills to conquer.

She approached the mare and tried to appear confident. It seemed to her this horse was slightly shorter than the others she'd ridden—or perhaps she was just taller now. Either way, it helped alleviate some of her anxiety. With a bright smile she took the reins and then stopped short at the sight of the saddle.

"Problem, Sophia?"

It was unlike any saddle she'd ever seen. There was no saddle horn, and the whole thing was covered with an unusual padded skin and then cinched again. "This is different."

"We keep to a gaucho saddle. It's not too difficult. I think you'll find it quite comfortable."

She resolutely put her toes in the stirrup and gripped the top of the saddle where she'd been hoping to find a saddle horn. On the second bounce she got it, and settled into the seat.

It felt different than the western saddles she remembered, but Tomas was right. It was fairly comfortable. The blanket cushioned her bottom.

With ease Tomas mounted up and flashed her a smile. "Neck rein, like in western riding," he instructed. "You do know how, right?"

Sophia resisted the impulse to bite down on her lip. It would be like learning all over again, but she would do it. After the spider incident of the morning, she would not let him see another weakness. This time she'd conquer her fear.

She put her right foot in the stirrup—somehow he'd managed to get the length just right—and with a nudge of her heels to the horse's side, followed him out of the corral and towards the sweeping plain surrounding the estancia.

For the first few minutes they kept to a nice, sedate walk. Sophia felt the breeze on her face and the sun on her back as they took the path through the maze of green pasture and pampas grass. Once the trail opened up, though, Tomas spurred his mount to a smooth canter and without any urging, Sophia's horse followed their lead.

The jolt of the motion and the unusual saddle nearly unseated her, but she gripped with her knees and after a few tense moments she settled into the rhythm of the stride. Not comfortably—she was too inexperienced for that—but she thought she might just manage to stay on top and not end up on her bottom in the dirt. Tomas slowed and eventually she caught up to him, fighting to control her breath and her heartbeat and act as though she did this every day of her life.

She envied Tomas. In comparison to her clumsiness and insecurity, he seemed as if he could do anything with ease. His hands held the reins loosely, unlike the death grip she seemed to have on the leather. His back was straight, his bearing almost regal. He looked like a god of the pampas up there, and the idea did funny things to her insides. For a woman so newly determined to be independent, the idea of having someone like Tomas as a protector was dizzying.

Oh, this was crazy. She was being romanced by the idea of some reticent cowboy and a South American version of the lawless West. She gave a small frown as she came back to earth. The distance she'd put between herself and her life back in Ottawa gave her perspective, and she knew she'd let herself be guided—pushed, molded, nudged—through life for too long. Did she even know who she was anymore? Wouldn't this week be a good time to find out?

"What do you think?"

Tomas reined in and swept his arm out in introduction to the wide, grassy plains below them. Cattle dotted the landscape, peacefully grazing. To their left, the stream the taxi had followed to the estancia twisted and wound like a silvery snake.

It reminded her of the rolling land she'd seen once when she had gone to Alberta for a student conference. As the bus had driven them from Calgary to Banff National Park, they'd passed rolling land like this, dotted with round bales of hay, horses and cattle. The estancia was a taste of that cowboy culture with a twist. There were no Stetsons and spurs here, but when Sophia looked over at Tomas, his brown eyes gleaming beneath his gaucho *campero*, she realized that some allures translated through language and location.

"It's gorgeous," she admitted, always aware of the animal beneath her, ready to adjust the tension of the reins if she needed to. "It's so open and free. Wild and a little intimidating."

Tomas got a little wrinkle in his brow. "You surprise me, Sophia. I expected more of a city-girl perspective from you."

"There are many things you don't know about me, Tomas," she remarked, pleased when the wrinkle got a little deeper. It was encouraging, knowing she had the ability to throw him a little off balance too. "You can be anything you want to be out here, can't you? There are no limits."

She saw him swallow and look away. "That's how I feel about it too. It is not so much frightening, but that there is a vastness to respect, *si?* I never knew what I was missing until I made friends with Miguel and he invited me to visit. The pampas…it is in my soul." He looked back at her, his gaze sharp and assessing. "Maybe being here all the time has made me forget that. It is good to see it through your eyes again."

"Then why don't you look happy?"

Sophia kept a firm grip on the reins as she watched Tomas's face. For a moment she thought he was going to say something, and then a muscle ticked in his jaw and she knew the moment had passed.

"This Miguel—he is Carlos and Maria's son?"

He nodded. "We became friends in university. An unlikely pair. Me from the city and him from the pampas."

Tomas laughed, but Sophia heard sadness behind it. "You weren't happy?"

"Maria and Carlos welcomed me like I was family. They were determined that Miguel have a better life. They might have been bitter about being poor, but instead they were just happy."

"And it isn't like that in your family?"

He laughed, but it sounded a bit forced. "No."

Sophia relaxed more in the saddle now, getting used to the shape and feel of it. "After she divorced my father, my mother was always very aware of the distinction of money... and the importance of opportunity. Hence my engagement to Antoine. A lawyer turned politician, full of money and ambition and the promise of power. He was everything she wanted in a son-in-law." In a flash of clarity, Sophia realized that her mother had wanted for her what she'd never quite had for herself. Sophia blinked, staring over the waving pampas grass, feeling some of her resentment fade as understanding dawned. "Mother just wanted security for me. When we announced our engagement, she was in heaven."

"And were you? In heaven?"

She thought back to the day she'd started working on Antoine's campaign staff. "I was dazzled for about thirty seconds. And then I was just practical. Antoine had a lot to offer. And he was charming and connected. He treated me well and I fancied myself in love with him, I suppose. We skated along and after a suitable amount of time he proposed. I would have a good life and he'd have a good wife for the campaign trail."

"Sounds passionate," he remarked dryly.

It hadn't been, and Sophia hoped she wasn't blushing. In this day and age it seemed unbelievable that in two years of dating and being engaged, she and Antoine had never slept together. Something had always held Sophia back. At the time she'd thought it sensible and cautious, considering how stories exploded through the news about the private lives of public people. Looking back now, though, she wondered if there hadn't been more to her decision she hadn't considered, if she hadn't put Antoine off for a bigger reason that even she hadn't understood. Looking at Tomas, feeling the thrill that zapped through her at the mere sight of him, she was beginning to see a glimmer of her reason. She'd overlooked an important ingredient—chemistry.

"Not exactly," she replied, staring out at the waving grasses. She'd blush again if she looked at Tomas. She was twenty-five years old and still a virgin. There was no way on earth she could say *that*.

"So, he was someone to keep you in shoes and handbags?" He tipped the brim of his hat back a little, his mischievous gaze settling on her face.

"Absolutely. More than that, it was stability." Something had changed between them. There was no malice in his accusation. She knew he was teasing, and she welcomed it. A teasing Tomas was far preferable to a grouchy one, even if his teasing did hit rather close to home at times. It was easier to take than the stares of disapproval. "Like Carlos and Maria, my mother was poor. My grandmother was a war bride from England and life on a Canadian farm wasn't all she'd dreamt it would be. She eventually divorced my grandfather. My mother fell into what she called the same trap, and she and my father split up when I was eight. Mom didn't handle poverty with the grace and humour of your friends, Tomas. She was alone. She was the one who made sure I had the opportunities and schooling and met all the right people."

Tomas nudged his mount forward, keeping the pace at a steady walk. "So you came here to throw it in your ex's face."

Had she? Perhaps in a way, but the trip had been far more about her than it had been about Antoine. "If I had wanted to throw it in his face, I would have gone to the media and given them all the details. It wasn't necessary. Calling off the wedding was damaging enough. Even without making an official statement, I had reporters in my face. It is big news when a high-profile party member is embroiled in a scandal—even if it's not quite clear what the scandal is." She angled him a wry smile and he smiled back.

"You're tougher than I thought," Tomas admitted. "Maybe I underestimated you, Sophia Hollingsworth."

"Maybe you did. But the real reason I came was because I was looking for someone."

He turned his head towards her again. "Who?"

A lump formed in Sophia's throat as she gripped the reins. The horse perked up at the feel of her hands through the leather.

"Me," she replied, and nudged the mare along and down the path leading to the creek.

CHAPTER FOUR

TOMAS followed her, his eyes trained on her back as it swayed gently with the motion of the horse. She had taken the initiative and started down the path before him, rather than follow behind. There was definitely more to Sophia than he thought. More than the designer shoes and air of supremacy she'd put on yesterday, or the panic she'd exhibited this morning during the spider episode. She was not experienced with horses. He'd known it from the start and had wanted to push her, test her. Not in a dangerous sort of way, after all he'd given her Neva, the gentlest mare in the stable. It was his job to gauge someone's experience and give them a proper mount. But he'd wanted to shake her up a bit. He'd nearly expected protests when she'd seen the gaucho saddle. But she hadn't said a single word. Just mounted and followed him.

She'd shown some pluck, and he liked that.

Maybe they had more in common than he'd thought. The thought niggled. He didn't want to find common ground. Maybe they had both felt pushed into a life of appearances. Tomas had lived that way once. For his father, money and status were everything. The biggest mistake of his life was going along with it as long as he had. He was far happier here, at Vista del Cielo.

Sophia just hadn't found her place yet, but it wasn't his job to show her. The words of assurance sat on his tongue but he remained silent, knowing that if he offered them to her, it would open him up to more questions. He wasn't sure where life was going to lead him and he didn't want to get into it with Sophia. Too many people offered their opinions as it was. As much as he loved it here on the estancia, his family kept asking when he was coming back. It was a question he could not answer. The idea of going back to Buenos Aires and taking his place at Motores Mendoza held little appeal. Lately he'd been feeling disconnected, and it unsettled him. Going back to Buenos Aires and the family business would sever that connection completely, and he couldn't do it.

"It is beautiful here," Sophia called from ahead of him. "So open and free." She reined in a bit so his horse's head was at her flank. "The big things melt away, don't they."

He exhaled slowly. Perhaps she was faking her riding experience, but there was no faking the approval he heard in her voice. "It does tend to put things in perspective," he replied carefully, pleased that she understood but still on his guard. Somehow the words tethered the two of them together, and that made him uncomfortable. "I have done a lot of thinking riding along this path." And he had, ever since the first visit when Miguel had brought him home to meet his family.

He'd walked in the door and everything in his world had changed. Everything. He had been greeted warmly. And he had laid eyes on Rosa and it was as though the world stopped turning.

The path grew steeper as they descended to the creek bed. She was being cautious, he noticed, knowing the *criollo* horses' nimble feet could more than handle the narrow path. At the bottom the mare gave a little hop and he heard a squeak come from ahead.

He watched the curve of Sophia's bottom as it swayed with the lazy stride of the mare. This morning he'd been sorely tempted to reach out and pull her into his arms when she'd seen the spider. Her alarm had been real, not put on, and he'd felt oddly protective of her. He shook his head. They would keep the pace slow, that was all.

A little further down the bed was a lee, sheltered from the wind. Tomas and Miguel had come here often to build a fire and share *mate*. He urged his horse forward and past Sophia, leading the way. If she didn't take a break, she would be sore in the morning from sitting in the saddle too long. This was the perfect place to rest. He had been here many times since coming to the estancia.

He dismounted and waited for her to follow, then tethered both horses to a low bush. "Come," he said, and held out a hand to help her over the scrabbly rocks. "I want to show you something."

She put her hand in his and his body tightened.

It was a trusting move and he hadn't expected the sweetness of it. The sharp-tongued cobra of yesterday had disappeared... when? When she'd come to the kitchen in her bare feet? This morning, when she'd blinked up at him in the baggy coveralls?

Her hand was small and soft and a lump formed in his throat. When was the last time someone had put their hand in his so trustingly? A long time. It bothered him that he couldn't remember. So many things he'd taken for granted and brushed off, not realizing how important they would become later. Things like the last time he had held Rosa's hand, kissed her lips. The last time he'd said "I love you" and heard her say his name. Those moments were gone forever, leaving a vacuum in their place.

They went to the curve in the hill where two flat rocks waited. "Oh!" she exclaimed, letting go of his hand and moving forward delightedly. Sophia went to the first stone and perched upon it, her hands on her knees.

She looked about eighteen years old. Where was the high fashion barracuda in stilettos demanding he make good on the reservation? It had been false bravado. He understood that now. The woman before him was an enchanting sprite with flaming curls and bright eyes. This was the real Sophia. Her excitement was fresh and genuine and far more difficult to resist.

"This is so neat! You can't even see it from above!"

"Which made it perfect for staying hidden." He followed her, moving towards the twin boulders, his boots crunching on the gravel.

"Who were you hiding from?"

"Mostly Carlos and Maria. Miguel and I would grab a couple of horses and come out. He was in a hurry to finish school and go to the city. I was dying to get out of the fast pace and expectations and this became my second home. He still loves it—I don't think you can take the pampas out of the boy. But he is working in Córdoba now, teaching at one of the universities."

He sat on the other stone and stared at the bubbling creek.

"Do you normally bring guests here on the trail rides? It's lovely."

"No, not usually." He suddenly knew this was a bad idea. The last thing he needed to do was start doing special things with her. She was no different than any other guest. She couldn't be.

"And so you have made your home with Maria and Carlos, working the estancia with them."

Tomas smiled. She made it sound so simple, when it wasn't. Not at all. He could tell her that he was joint owner, but for some reason he didn't want to.

"I prefer it to being with my own family. I know, that sounds awful, as if I don't love them. And I know in my way I do. But what you said before, about looking for someone...I understand that. It is when I am here that I feel most myself. If somehow a trip here is managing to give that to you, too, I'm glad. Sometimes..." He thought about what she'd told him only minutes before. "Sometimes being here I remember I don't have to try so hard."

They were quiet for a few moments. He looked over at Sophia. She was gazing out over the creek and the waving grasses, her expression utterly relaxed, her hands resting on her knees.

"I know what you mean about trying hard out here. It's beautiful, isn't it? I didn't think so when I first drove up. It wasn't what I was expecting. But now I think perhaps the estancia is well named. View of Heaven...yes. I think your pampas might have a way of winding itself around a person's heart."

And just like that, Sophia started winding herself around *him*. She understood what it was he felt about the pampas, about Vista del Cielo. It was the last thing he expected and the sensation was pleasant and disturbing all at once.

"I think I've been trying hard for a long time," she continued. "To please people. To be what they wanted me to be. I don't even really know what I want."

He nodded. "But you have time. You're what, twenty-four, twenty-five?" He traced a fingernail over the rock's surface. "This is a whole new beginning for you. You get to decide who you want to be."

Her smile was wide. "Thank you, Tomas." She tipped her *campero* back further on her head. "I sometimes worry that I've taken this trip for revenge. It's not a very attractive quality. After what you just said...I hope that instead I use it as a springboard for doing things better." He saw a glimmer of moisture in her eyes. "Living honestly, if that makes sense."

Oh, it made sense all right. And at least her catastrophe was only a cancelled wedding. She had no need of the remorse that Tomas still felt about his own personal wake-up call.

"Anyway," she changed the subject lightly, "I am looking forward to meeting Maria and Carlos." She stretched out her legs and tilted her face up to the sun.

"You will like them," he answered quietly.

"Do you suppose their son will ever have children? Is he married? My grandmother always joked that grandchildren were the bane of her existence. She didn't like kids any more than she liked farm life." Sophia chuckled.

Tomas did not know how to answer. She was just making simple chatter, but the subject of grandchildren was a painful one. As the silence stretched out, he searched for a safe topic of conversation. He thought about giving her a spiel on the history of the gaucho but suspected she'd see clear through his motive to deflect the conversation away from himself. "Or maybe you." She kept on, oblivious to the sickening churning he was feeling in his gut. "Maybe you will have children and will bring them out here to visit."

The innocently spoken words were like a knife in his heart.

He and Rosa had sneaked out to this spot on occasion too. If he had been any other boy, Carlos and Maria would have had a fit. But not with Tomas. They had trusted him to take care of Rosa. To keep her safe and cherish her. Sophia's words were nothing that he had not thought of a million times since Rosa's death. Time, and yes, even healing, could not erase the awful responsibility he felt.

"Tomas?"

He hadn't noticed her rising from her rock and coming to his side. Her small hand lay on his forearm and when he turned his head she was watching him, her dark eyes wide and worried. Her skin was creamy and her hair was a mass of flaming waves. But it was the concern, the gentle way she touched him and his reaction to it that caused pain and resentment to rip through his insides.

"Did I say something wrong?"

He shook his head, knowing she was not to blame. It was him, all him. *Take a breath,* he commanded himself. Sophia was a guest. That was all. He should still be grieving. He shouldn't be thinking of her this way.

"I think it is time we got back. I wanted to get the boxes moved into the boutique this afternoon."

She bit down on her lip and his gaze was drawn to it, unerringly, inevitably. Soft and pink, it regained its shape as her teeth released it.

He got up from the rock and straightened, staring unseeingly at the creek. He would not touch her. He would not kiss her or take her in his arms.

"Why do you shut people out all the time, Tomas? Or is it just me? For a few moments I think you're going to relax and then you wrap yourself in layers again."

She was right, and he refused to respond. What could he possibly say that would be appropriate? That he was contemplating how soft her skin might be beneath her blouse? The only thing he could do was remain silent.

"Did she hurt you that badly?" Sophia pressed him. "I asked about you before, but maybe it was the other way around. Did someone cheat on you the way that Antoine cheated on me?"

"What?" He swung his head around. "No. Never!"

But the question had revealed a chink in his armor. "So there was someone else," Sophia prodded.

She would not let this go, and what had begun as a relaxing afternoon changed into something painful and raw. Why was he finding it so hard to treat her like a guest? He should be pointing out landforms and local history and instead they were talking about failed relationships. How had he lost control so easily? How had she managed to get under his skin?

She thought he was some romantic gaucho figure, someone honorable and upright. But he wasn't. She had to stop looking at him this way—with a soft understanding, as if she knew... She didn't know.

He'd made peace with what had happened. He'd accepted

the blame. And he'd moved on to the kind of life he'd wanted, throwing himself into developing the estancia. Good, honest, put-your-back-into-it work. So why did Sophia have to show up now and make him want things he had no right wanting?

Two days. Two days and Maria and Carlos would be back. His duty would be discharged and he could be back behind the scenes where he belonged.

He retrieved Sophia's horse and brought the mare to her, holding the reins while she used the height of the rock to get her feet in the stirrups. "Hold her steady," he commanded, going to get his gelding and swinging up into the saddle.

Even with her own set of troubles, he still saw Sophia as naive. She'd had a rude awakening with this Antoine, but he knew deep down she still believed in a forever kind of love. In happily-ever-afters. Tomas had known for a long time how the world worked. Those who succeeded at love and marriage and happiness...they were just lucky. The majority of people wandered through life trying to figure out how they'd gotten so lost.

"Let's get back," he said tersely, nudging his horse forward and up the hardened slope. They needed to move on before he said something he'd really regret.

Like the truth.

Sophia gripped the reins in fingers slippery from the afternoon heat. Her thighs already ached from exercising unused muscles. She nudged the mare with her heels and followed Tomas up the slope and on to the level table of the pampas. He was already a bit ahead, and Sophia gritted her teeth.

She had done just fine during the first part of the ride, so she nudged the mare into a trot and hoped for the best. First he had clammed up when she'd asked a simple question. Now he had deliberately gone ahead and he hadn't looked back to check on her once. That particular fact agitated her. His bossiness was just another way of keeping that stoic, annoying distance. If he thought he could shake her that easily, that he could just ride off without another word, he had another think coming.

Her thighs burned as she tried to hold on to the saddle. *Don't let me fall off,* she prayed as she jounced along at a trot. Finally she caught up with Tomas.

"You might have waited."

Tomas looked over, his dark eyes shaded by his *campero*. Sophia felt a momentary flash of annoyance and attraction together, which only served to irritate her further. She should not find him attractive at all. He was a closed-mouthed, stubborn man who kept setting her up to fail. She was just about to tell him so when a puff of wind stirred up a dust devil in front of them.

Tomas's gelding shied and Tomas quickly settled him, but Sophia's mare took a scare and bolted, Sophia clinging helplessly to saddle and reins. Hooves pounded against the earth. She tried to keep her posture, but her feet bounced in the stirrups, bumping against the mare's side, unintentionally prodding her to go faster. Then Sophia heard Tomas shout in Spanish as the mare leapt forward, heading straight for the estancia at breakneck speed.

Sweat poured down her spine now and she could see the gate in front of her. If they didn't slow down soon...

Tomas shouted again. Desperately she pulled on the reins but their length was uneven in her damp palms and the mare shifted abruptly to her right. Everything seemed to slow as she felt the horse plant its feet, throwing her from the saddle. There was a sense of weightlessness as she flew through the air and a fear in knowing she was likely to be hurt.

When Sophia hit the ground, every last breath of air was forced from her lungs and she felt several seconds of panic as they refused to work. Finally new oxygen rushed in, painful and a blessed relief all in one.

Tomas reined in beside her and jumped off his horse, leaving the reins dangling from the bridle.

"Sophia!" Tomas knelt beside her and she felt his hands behind her shoulders as she tried to sit. "No, lie down," he commanded, gently placing her on the grass. "Catch your breath, and tell me you're all right."

His face swam before her eyes as she inhaled and exhaled, trying to steady her breathing to somewhat near normal even though her chest felt as though someone was stepping on it. Lying down helped. Tomas's hat was on the grass beside them and she saw a slight ring around his scalp where the band and sweat had flattened his short dark curls. He was beautiful, she realized. In an unreal sort of way—dark and mysterious and perfect. She felt horribly dirty, provincial and awkward. She'd tried to fake knowing what she was doing, but she'd been unequal to the task, just as she'd been at painting this morning. She'd failed yet again. All she'd had to do was stay in the saddle for another fifteen minutes and she would have been home free.

Now she looked like a prize idiot next to Tomas's stunning looks, self assurance and…

Oh Lord. The way he was looking at her right now. Like he *cared*. His lips were unsmiling, his eyes dark with anxiety. How long had she wished for someone to look at her in just this way? As though if something happened to her it would be a catastrophe? Antoine certainly never had. He'd acted as if her feelings, her needs, counted for nothing.

And counting for nothing hurt, dammit. She finally acknowledged to herself that Antoine's betrayal of her had hurt most because she had felt inconsequential. Had felt that she didn't matter.

Tomas's hand reached behind her head and cradled it in his hand, cushioning it from the hard earth. "Sophia, please," he said roughly. "Tell me where it hurts."

His plea broke through every defence she'd erected since

walking into the hotel room and seeing Antoine with his mistress. Her whole life hurt right now. She had never felt so alone. And the worst part of it was that she knew she couldn't make sense of any of it until she figured out who she was. It was a horrible, horrible feeling to realize that she'd lost herself along the way. She was like a boat bobbing aimlessly on the sea with no direction. And it had taken this rough-and-ready gaucho to make her see it. Maybe she'd looked like a fool just now, but there was no mistaking the genuine concern in his eyes. She held on to that, letting it be a beacon in the darkness.

I hurt everywhere, she thought, and she felt the telltale sting of tears behind her eyes. And the last thing she wanted was for him to see that. She'd lost enough face today.

She gripped his forearm with her hand and pulled herself up to sit.

"It's my fault," Tomas berated himself sharply. "I never should have gone off ahead. I knew you were inexperienced." He brushed a piece of hair off her cheek and tucked it behind her ear. "You were doing wonderfully. You have more pluck than I gave you credit for."

Sophia's face softened. Did Tomas blame himself? That was ridiculous. He couldn't have known the mare would run off.

"I'm fine," she insisted, knowing that nothing was broken, only bruised. There was an ache in her hip from landing on the hard ground, and she suspected she would be stiff later, but the greatest harm had been done to her pride. And yet his words stirred something warm inside. Had he actually said she'd been doing wonderfully? She had been faking the whole way, trying to remember what she'd learned about riding in those two childhood rides. So she hadn't fooled him. But she hadn't made a disaster of it, either. At least not until the end.

"At least you know I never do things halfway," she replied.

She looked around. Both horses were standing a few metres away, looking utterly unconcerned about Sophia's welfare. Her *campero* had flown off and was lying in the dust.

"Don't move," he ordered, and he went to the horses, gathering the reins and tethering them to the fence. He snagged her hat and came back, sliding an arm under her knees and picking her up while the *campero* dangled from his fingers. Her breath hitched as he stood and gave a little bounce, adjusting her weight in his arms.

"What are you doing?"

"Carrying you inside, what do you think?"

It was heavenly being in his arms, the primitive physicality of it thrilling. She was held closely against the wall of his chest, so close that she could see a single bead of sweat gather at the hollow of his throat. She wanted to reach out and touch it with the tip of her finger, but didn't have the courage to take such initiative.

He began carrying her towards the house. No man had ever done such a gallant thing for her before, and it would be very easy to get swept away. But this was definitely not standing on her own two feet and the last thing she wanted was to look like some helpless female. She'd done that enough today. "Please, put me down. I can walk."

"You took quite a fall, Sophia." His chocolatey eyes were still heavy with concern and a tiny wrinkle marred his brow.

Her arms had gone around his neck by instinct and her body bobbed with every long stride of his legs. "Then let me walk it off. Nothing is broken, Tomas. This is silly."

They reached the gate and she stuck out a hand, grabbing on to the metal bar and pulling them to a halt. "Let me down. You can walk me to the house if you want." His gaze caught hers for long seconds. "The fault is mine. I felt I had something to prove, but I was wrong. I should have asked for help. I didn't mean to scare you," she apologized.

He gave in and gently put her down. "Are you sure you're not hurt?"

She did hurt. She missed the feeling of being held in his arms already, and she ached all over. Her left hip pained when she put her weight on it. But it was just bruising. "Nothing serious. I'm more humiliated than anything."

They took slow steps to the house. Tomas remained right by her side, slowing his strides to match hers, his right arm always near in case she needed support. "I'm the one who should apologize, Sophia. You are inexperienced with horses, and I knew that. This is all my fault. I should not have ridden ahead."

"Why did you?" She hobbled along, looking up at him from beneath her *campero,* the hat resting crookedly atop her head.

"I…"

"You're going to put that wall around yourself again, aren't you? Fine. I get it. You are allowed to ask questions. I'm not. Loud and clear, Tomas."

"*Dios,* your tongue is sharp!" He bristled beside her. "You might have been killed, do you understand? What if Neva had gone down? What if she'd rolled on you?"

He turned on her, anger darkening his face now. "I should have stayed with you. You might have broken your neck."

"Oh, what would you care? You'll be glad to be rid of me, admit it!" she shot back. She instantly felt bad for saying it. "Tomas, I'm…"

But he never gave her a chance.

"*¡Maldita idiota!* I cannot figure you out. You panic at the sight of a spider, but when the danger is real…"

"Perhaps you should have thought of that before giving me a skittish horse that runs at the least little thing!"

"I gave you the calmest horse in the stable!" They were standing in the middle of the yard now, shouting.

"Do you treat all your clients this way?" She scoffed, her

voice ripe with derision. Her blood was up now and it felt marvelous! All the righteous anger she'd channeled into cancelling the wedding and reorganizing her life came bubbling to the surface. "Oh wait...I'm the only one. Remind me why that is again?"

"¡Cállate!" He shouted. "Enough!"

And then he gripped her arms in his strong hands and kissed her.

The pain in her hip disappeared as his lips covered hers. Passion, a passion she hadn't known she even possessed, exploded within her and she reached out to hang on to his shirt. He braced his feet, forming a solid wall for her to lean against, and in return she twined her arms around his ribs and over his shoulder blades, craving the feel of his body against hers.

This was what had been missing, she realized with a shock. Pure, unadulterated physicality. The kind of force that rushed in like a hurricane and frightened the hell out of her.

She shuddered and the fingers gripping her arms eased. His mouth gentled over hers until his lips played, teased, seduced.

It made her want to weep. How was it that even in anger this stranger seemed to know exactly what she needed? How did he know that she needed gentleness?

"Are you still angry at me?" she whispered as their lips parted. She couldn't make herself meet his gaze; instead she stared at his mouth as though she hadn't seen it before. Full lips, crisp in their perfection, soft when they needed to be soft, firm when they needed to be commanding...

"Yes," he admitted, letting out a ragged breath. "Are you still angry at me?"

"No."

"Why?"

She sighed. "Because I'm tired of being angry."

"I shouldn't have shouted. You scared me, Sophia."

"I scared myself."

She risked a look up at him then. His eyes were dark with concern again and she marveled at it—why should he care about her? Who was she to him? But she wasn't about to argue. At the moment, sad as it was, he was all she had.

He turned from her and they began walking towards the house again. Sophia's legs felt like jelly after the kiss, but she forced one foot ahead of the other.

"Why didn't you say anything earlier when I mentioned going riding?"

"I didn't want you to know." She raised her chin. "After the way I showed up yesterday, and then my overreaction this morning...I didn't want you to think I was some vapid female who couldn't handle as much as a broken nail. I didn't expect to be racing across the pampas, either."

She wouldn't look at him, but to her right, she heard a soft chuckle. "You are very stubborn, Sophia Hollingsworth."

"Thank you. I'll take that as a compliment."

This time he really did laugh, and the sound reached in and expanded inside her. She knew it was ridiculous. She had made a miscalculation and now she was limping back to the house, dirty and with dented pride claiming that stubbornness was an attribute and not a fault.

"I didn't foresee that happening. I was a very poor tour guide today. If nothing else, I should have asked you about your experience instead of assuming."

"And what would you have done differently? Stop blaming yourself." She stopped and put a hand on his arm. His solicitousness was lovely, but it wasn't required. "It was the wind, that's all." Her body warmed as their kiss was still foremost in her mind. "And...about what happened before...I don't want you to fix things, Tomas. I came on this holiday to be my *own* solution. Please don't take this as an insult. I'm coming to understand I have spent far too long being at the mercy of other people. I need to prove to myself that I am capable, too."

"And just what did this afternoon prove?" He raised an eyebrow, challenging.

They were at the house now and Sophia paused with her hand on the door.

What did it prove? Perhaps that the appreciation she had for Tomas had blossomed into full-blown attraction. And it had proved that the feeling was mutual. The potential in that stopped her in her tracks. It was an exhilarating, terrifying thought.

She took a careful breath. "It proved I am in dire need of a hot bath. And perhaps a glass of wine."

"I think the Vista del Cielo can handle that."

But Tomas waited a moment before backing away. "Are you sure you're okay? I can call a doctor." His hand rested on her shoulder and she tried not to like the heat of it there— but she did anyway. She could protest all she wanted, but it felt good to be cared for, taken care of, even just a little. The simple touch made her wonder what it would be like if he came inside with her, maybe kissed her again. Would it be as good the second time? Better?

"Truly, I'm fine, thank you." She didn't want him to leave. She wanted to see him smile, and feel the way his gaze fell on her, warm and approving in the Argentine sun. She wanted him to touch her cheeks with his lips again and maybe slide that small distance to her mouth. Her gaze fell unerringly on his lips too and then back up to his eyes. She'd give up her soak in the bath for that.

"I will see you later. I must look after the horses if you are all right."

"I'm not going anywhere."

She wasn't going anywhere, not yet. But in another week she would be on a plane headed back to Canada. That much would not change no matter how enamored she became of her surroundings. She took one last approving look at his retreating figure. *All* of her surroundings.

CHAPTER FIVE

"WHAT are you doing?" Tomas asked, stepping into the kitchen. He'd spent a long time in the barns, avoiding Sophia after their kiss. Needing to clear his mind. It hadn't worked. The taste and feel of her stayed with him until there was no more tack left to polish. He'd put things off a little longer by having a quick shower. Now he'd come to the kitchen to scrounge something to eat, never expecting to find Sophia there. He'd figured she'd be exhausted from her eventful day.

"Making dinner. You were busy in the barn, and I was cleaned up, so…" she broke off the sentence, turning around to face him as she wiped her hands on a towel. "I didn't know what sort of food you were used to, so I put together a cold meal. I hope that's okay."

Tomas stepped forward, just enough to catch the perfumed scent of her skin. She should have been dead on her feet after the extraordinary day they'd had. Instead he found her here looking like an ad in a magazine. She wore a dress that managed to hug her figure yet appear elegant, drawing his gaze to the soft curve of her hips. Her hair was up in some sort of twist that looked simple and casual and that he expected took a great deal of talent to arrange. Silver and amethyst earrings dangled at her ears. And the shoes were back. Lower heels this time, but he raised his eyebrows at the sandals that blended shades of pink, lime green and turquoise. They should have been garish. Instead, they complemented everything, making her look young and stylish.

Like the woman who had arrived yesterday. Tomas knew he should be relieved. It was easier to distance himself from her when she looked like this—foreign and out of his league.

But he missed how her eyes had glittered up at him from beneath her *campero* and how cuddly she'd appeared in his coveralls. "You didn't have to make dinner."

"But you said everyone pitches in. I ditched you earlier— literally. And my bath was very refreshing. I fear today's activities have left me starving."

She smiled up at him and he felt his breath catch. This was wrong. It was purely physical. But it was just attraction. Nothing more. He could handle it. Another few days and she'd be gone. Just a blip on the libido radar until things got back to normal.

"How is your hip?" he enquired politely, ignoring the way his pulse had quickened and moving to help with the prepara- tions. She'd already laid out a selection of cold meats from the fridge, as well as cheese and sliced vegetables. The food was placed strategically on a platter, in sections and precise layers that made it a work of art.

"Sore, but the bath helped, and the scented salts, too. They are a lovely addition to the room, Tomas. It should be men- tioned to Maria. A nice touch." She put the last few slices of tomato in place and stood back. "There. All that is missing is slicing the bread."

"I can do that. You should get off your feet." Tomas felt off balance at the change in their conversation. In some ways it felt polite and distant, and yet there was a comfortableness to it that made it seem that they'd known each other far longer than a couple of days. And then there was the kiss that neither of them had mentioned. It stood between them, a lump of something that was hard to ignore. They had both retreated to their respective corners since then, looking for solid footing. Had it affected her as strongly as it had him?

He sliced the bread and Sophia laid it on a plate around a small bowl of herbed butter. "Let's eat outside," Tomas suggested. He wouldn't feel so closed in if they ate in the backyard. "I can light a fire. We often do in the evenings."

"That would be lovely." Again she smiled, warm and polite, and Tomas got the sneaky suspicion that it was her friendly meet-the-politician smile.

It was no more than he deserved, and he should be glad she'd taken a step back. But he hated it.

They carried the food outdoors, and while Sophia went back into the kitchen to retrieve a bottle of wine and glasses, Tomas began laying a fire.

This formality was exactly what he'd wanted. So why did it feel so awkward?

After the meal he insisted on doing the cleaning up and sent Sophia to rest her hip. When the last dish was dry and back in the cupboard, he found her in the living room, curled into a corner of the sofa, sleeping.

She looked so innocent with her lashes on her cheeks and her lips relaxed in slumber. Her shoes were on the floor and her dress had slid up her thigh, revealing the soft skin to his gaze. Gently, so as not to wake her, he ran his finger up the smooth length, stopping at the hem and drawing back. He didn't know what to make of her. One moment fragile, the next stubborn as a mule. Today he'd felt he'd let her down. He knew she could have been seriously injured, and he'd expected her to retreat to spoiled form. But instead she'd risen above it and had proved her mettle.

He reached out and touched her shoulder, and as her eyes opened and focused on his he felt the burning start, deep in his gut.

"It's time for bed," he said quietly.

For a few moments something hummed between them.

The memory of the afternoon's kiss seemed to sizzle in the air. Her eyes had the same hooded, dazed look now as they'd had then, and he swallowed, resisting the urge to reach out and run his thumb over her cheekbone.

He had the most irrational thought of taking her down the hall to the family quarters and tucking her beneath his sheets before crawling in beside her and holding her close. Her dark eyes showed the slightest hint of alarm as if she understood the direction of his thoughts even though no words had been spoken.

But that was wrong, and crazy, and definitely not what Maria had meant when she'd ordered him to look after their guest. He stepped back and cleared his throat.

"Sleep well, Sophia," he said, and gathering all his willpower, walked down the hallway alone.

Sophia dug in her pitchfork, wrinkled her nose and, holding her breath, deposited the soiled straw in the wheelbarrow.

When she'd heard Tomas rise this morning, she'd hurriedly hopped out of bed and pulled on the *bombachas* of yesterday. She would not be late. She was determined not to lag. She put her hand on her still-aching hip. She'd show Tomas she was made of sterner stuff. Last night she'd been exhausted and still reeling from Tomas's kiss. Putting on the dress and shoes and making dinner was the best way to keep her guard up, to show him a tumble from a horse would not defeat her. And neither would a most heavenly kiss from her sexy gaucho. What she wanted and how far she was prepared to go were two very different things.

The kiss had nearly been repeated before bed last night. She had seen it in his eyes, and for a few seconds she had leaned the slightest bit towards him, her nerve endings on high alert. In the end he'd backed away. She should have been relieved. Would he expect her to be a woman of the world? She knew she was an anomaly—a virgin at her age. The pull to him was undeniable, but her hesitancy was equally strong.

She'd lain awake a long time thinking about it, and this morning she'd awakened tired but more determined than ever to pull her weight. To prove that she was up to any challenge he could throw at her.

But that was before she'd realized that the first chores of the morning were mucking out stalls and feeding the horses. Now Tomas had turned the stock out into a nearby pasture to graze while they shoveled manure. There was no other polite way to put it. She put another forkful in the barrow as Tomas strode up the corridor whistling. It was obscenely early to sound so cheerful. When she saw his boots stop beside her, she turned with a scoop of dirty straw and was deliberately careless so that a bit fell on his boots with a plop.

Then, calm as you please, she deposited the rest in the wheelbarrow.

"Thank you for your help this morning," Tomas said, shaking off his foot, unconcerned. "You're really getting into the swing of things now, aren't you?"

The sun was barely up and Sophia was dying for a first cup of coffee, and the sooner they finished the sooner she could have it. But despite the unpalatable chore, the dew on the grass and the early morning birdsong somehow made everything rosier. "It's not so bad."

He took the pitchfork from her hand. "I'll get rid of this. There's fresh straw over there to put in the stalls."

Sophia spent the next fifteen minutes putting down the layer of straw, all the while listening to Tomas's cheerful whistling. After the hours she'd spent puzzling out what exactly their kiss had meant, Tomas was acting as if nothing had happened at all. She shook out the last of the straw and dusted off her hands.

"Are you ready for breakfast?" Tomas came back around the corner and Sophia straightened, bracing her lower back with both hands. There had been a communion to working with him this morning. A satisfaction of working together, much like that she'd felt yesterday as they'd painted the shed. Her stomach grumbled and Tomas smiled at her. "I'll take that as a yes."

She followed him back to the house as the sun peeked over the rolling hills, colouring the pampas with a fresh, warm glow. She inhaled deeply, enjoying the open space that was at once youthful and timeless. Each day started anew, with the flaws of yesterday behind it. As they reached the door she closed her eyes and let out a breath. Antoine, her mom, her friends—they would be appalled at the fact that she'd spent her first daylight hours cleaning a dirty horse barn. And yes, it had been an unusual experience. But not a bad one.

As she and Tomas pulled off their boots, Sophia realized she was perhaps made of more than she was given credit for. Perhaps she simply hadn't tried because it had been safer that way. Secure. No risk, no loss.

"What's so funny?" Tomas's voice broke through her thoughts as he went to the sink to wash up. She joined him there, sharing the soap as they washed their hands beneath the running water.

"Two days ago when I arrived, I didn't plan on shoveling... well, you know."

"You did a fine job for a beginner."

She dried her hands and gave him the towel. "Thank you, but now I want to know what's to eat. All that fresh air has given me an appetite." She would kill for bacon and eggs, the sort of breakfast that never passed her lips anymore. Perhaps it was the combination of hard work and fresh air. Perhaps it was knowing that she need not hold to the conventions of the past at Vista del Cielo. Either way, she was famished.

As if he read her mind, Tomas took eggs from the fridge. "I will fry some eggs and there is the bread from yesterday."

Her mouth watered at the thought of a fried-egg sandwich. "That sounds perfect."

They worked together to prepare the meal, and once they sat at the table Tomas asked, "How's the hip?"

Sophia chewed and swallowed. It still pained, but she didn't want it to keep her from whatever Tomas had planned for the day. Now that she had made a success of something, she wanted to build on the momentum. The sense of accomplishment was addictive. "It's a little sore, but I'm no worse for the wear."

"Since the chores are done, I thought you might like a trip into town. You can find some clothes there, perhaps some souvenirs to take back home with you."

"What about the shed? We still have to put on another coat of paint." But Tomas shook his head.

"I decided it can wait. We should be back later this afternoon and I can paint it then."

"Are you sure?"

Tomas swiped his bread across his plate. "Yes, I'm sure. You helped this morning. It is your vacation after all. If Maria were here, she would take you on a day trip to town. In her absence, it's my job."

Sophia felt her excitement deflate. This was nothing more than Tomas living up to his responsibilities once again. Making up for yesterday, too, she supposed. It had nothing to do with actually *wanting* to spend time with her. It was his duty. His job.

Still, a day in town sounded fun. She didn't want to spend her whole trip on the estancia. She wanted to see new things. And perhaps she could purchase some comfortable clothes. But first she'd have to have a shower to get rid of the barn smell.

"Just give me twenty minutes to clean up."

Back in Canada, it would have taken her three times that

long to be ready for a day out. Sophia smiled as she took her plate to the sink.

In Argentina, nothing was the same.

"Me, too," Tomas replied. As Sophia went back to her room to gather fresh clothing, she told herself she would not think about Tomas's dark, lean body beneath the shower spray.

Sophia's feet were beginning to ache from all the walking, but it had been worth it. She wiped her lips with a paper napkin and then crumpled it, tossing it into a nearby garbage bin. They'd stopped at a sausage cart for lunch, grabbing a snack to tide them over before heading back to the estancia for the afternoon. The chorizo had been suitably spicy and the bread chewy and fresh. Beside her, Tomas gave a satisfied sigh and she smiled.

"That was delicious."

"Not fancy, but one of my favourites." He too wiped his mouth and disposed of the napkin.

The afternoon was hot and Sophia soaked in the heat, enjoying the feel of it on her skin. Tomas had proven a better tour guide than she'd expected. They'd spent the morning visiting the Gaucho Museum and browsing the silver shops, admiring the craftsmanship. She'd bought two casual outfits and a pair of silver earrings for her mother as a gift. Meanwhile, Tomas had taken her to a local *bodega* where he'd picked up several bottles of Malbec, claiming it was Maria's particular favourite. Once they'd stowed their packages in the estancia's SUV, he'd suggested a quick lunch of grilled sausage wrapped in a bun. It had been perfect. They had munched while walking along the river. Now, with the shops closing for the afternoon, they ambled along the pathway.

A group of boys were playing soccer ahead, their shouts a happy sound in the peaceful quiet. "This is such a lovely town," Sophia said. "Honestly, Tomas, the more I see you here the more I understand. I'm a city girl, where things are vibrant and rush, rush, rush. But here, it's…" She broke off, confused. "It's hard to explain."

But Tomas nodded. "That's what staying at the Vista del Cielo is all about, remember? Maybe sometimes I take the quiet and slower pace for granted."

He paused and faced her, taking her hands in his. "Sophia…"

He stopped and his jaw tightened. His fingers clasped hers tightly as she looked up into his face, falling under the spell of his dark gaze as her heart began to pound. Did he possibly know how attractive he was, how magnetic? They didn't even have to be close to one another for her to feel the pull. It had been there yesterday, too, even as they'd shouted at each other.

But now, as he held her hands in his, she couldn't help but wonder what it would be like to throw caution to the wind and take things a step further. A holiday romance had been the very last thing on her mind when she'd left Canada. But faced with Tomas… The trouble was that he wasn't just a sexy, enigmatic gaucho anymore. She knew what it was like to see him smile. Her heart still caught when she remembered the look in his eyes as he'd cradled her head in his hand yesterday, asking if she was all right.

And her body practically sang at the memory of feeling his lips on hers. She couldn't deny the possibility of a brief romance held a certain allure. But as soon as she thought it, she dismissed it. What if she flirted? Tried to get him to kiss her again? Then what? What would he expect? Maybe nothing. But maybe a whole lot more than she was comfortable with. In some ways, she'd already bitten off more than she could chew with this trip. Tempting Tomas might definitely turn into more than she could handle, and if she were honest with herself, she just wasn't ready.

"Is there something you want to say?" She gave his fingers a gentle squeeze.

For a long moment his gaze plumbed hers, but then he released her hands. "Just…it seems strange to be saying this, but seeing your view of the town, the pampas…" He paused, then offered a small smile, just a faint curving of his lips that reached out and held her in its grasp. "I had forgotten how to appreciate it," he said. "Thank you."

"Me? I've done nothing. I know I came across as a bit of a princess, Tomas…"

His warm chuckle sent tingles down her arms.

"I'm really not. Not deep down."

He looked as if he wanted to say something, but instead merely inclined his head towards the path. "Let's walk."

And there he went again, poking his head out of his shell just a little bit before turtling in again. It frustrated her even though she knew it was probably for the best.

They resumed walking along the path. "I'm afraid I haven't been very good company. I hope Carlos and Maria don't plan on using me as a tour guide very often."

"Don't be silly. I arrived unexpectedly and threw a monkey wrench into your week."

"You're our guest, Sophia."

He'd said *our* and not *my* and Sophia felt the difference. She watched the boys kick the ball around, one rushing in to score a victorious goal. Another boy, smaller, scuffed his toe on the ground in frustration. Sophia knew how that felt. It was like trying to gain Tomas's approval. It was a rare commodity, and somehow she felt it was worth striving for. A romance was out of the question. There was so much potential for things to go wrong. But she somehow wanted to think that they were friends of a sort. Someone who was a friend to the new and improved Sophia.

"I…I'd like to think maybe we're friends," she said quietly.

"Friends?" he asked, and she heard the surprise in his voice. Didn't he have friends? Was it so incomprehensible?

"Sure," she smiled as their steps slowed even further.

"*Amigos.* I mean, you know more about me than you normally would about a guest, right? Far more than 'where are you from, what do you do?'"

"I suppose."

But did friends get that twirling of anticipation from simply knowing they were going to be together? She knew they didn't. There was more between them. The question was, were they going to ignore it or explore it? Which did she really want? This was supposed to be a simple trip, uncomplicated. And Tomas was one big sexy complication.

They kept on until they reached the *Puente Viejo,* a gorgeous salmon-pink bridge spanning the river. They stood at the crest of it and rested their arms on the ledge, looking down at the smooth water.

"Sophia," Tomas began, and she looked up at him, surprised to see his brows pulled together in a pensive frown when they were in one of the most beautiful, relaxing places she could remember.

"What is it?"

"As friends, I feel I should apologize for kissing you yesterday."

"It has bothered you," she acknowledged. Was this why he'd spent hours in the barn rather than coming to the house? Was it why he'd brought her to town today? Guilt?

"I was very out of line yesterday, Sophia. You gave me such a scare. I fear my actions made you uncomfortable."

Oh yes. In the most heart-stopping, glorious way, but there was no way she was going to tell him that. Especially when he clearly didn't feel the same. With Tomas it was always duty first. She could resent him for that if it weren't so darned admirable.

"It's okay, Tomas." Sophia forced a smile when she felt none. "I know it was just a reaction. The fall scared us both. I know it wasn't real."

Tomas didn't respond and the silence was more awkward

than any words might have been. Was there any clearer confirmation? She needed to say something, something to dispel the tense atmosphere. Was Tomas thinking about it as she was? Clearly he regretted it. He was not interested in her. She, on the other hand, was remembering the kiss quite differently. She was feeling quite giddy about it, which wouldn't do at all.

"I'm afraid I'm not a great host," Tomas said, relaxing just a little. Sophia supposed clearing the air about the kiss was a relief to him. Tomas linked his fingers together over the railing. "Maria is much better at this sort of thing. She knows how to make people at home."

What would Maria say if she knew Tomas had held Sophia in his arms? Or that Sophia had kissed him back as though she was dying of thirst and he was cool, reviving water?

"She'd flay me alive," Tomas continued, almost as if he'd heard Sophia's question. "For letting you take a fall like that."

"It sounds like she cares about you. As a mother would."

He laughed then, quietly, but it was warm and heartfelt, and Sophia loved how it changed his face.

"Maria is the heart and soul that keeps *this* family together," he said easily. "I'm afraid of what she'd say if she saw you. She'd be meddling in the first five minutes."

"Why?"

This time when Tomas met her gaze, he said nothing, but then he didn't have to. The memory of their kiss was suddenly front and centre again, the diversion shattered. "Do you have experience with meddling mothers?" Tomas said it quietly, his magnetic gaze never leaving hers, with tacit acknowledgement that they were attempting to change the subject.

Which made the attraction they were trying to ignore simmer all the stronger.

Sophia forced a laugh. "Are you kidding? My mother is the biggest meddler of them all. She was the one that introduced me to Antoine. And she pushed me into a country club wedding."

"Don't all girls want a fancy wedding?" Tomas stood tall and turned to face her, resting against the bridge.

She shook her head. "Not all girls. I didn't. Not a big production with two hundred guests, a photographer and a champagne fountain. I would have chosen something far simpler."

"I still find it hard to believe this Antoine let you get away."

"Oh, he didn't. He just thought he could have everything," she replied. And he had. Antoine had never considered that he would get caught. And even if he had, the expectation was that she'd fall in line just as she always did.

"It's made me think about my gram a lot," Sophia admitted. "Gram hated her life on the farm. She'd had a very different childhood in England. But I don't think she ever got over leaving her husband. He was the right man in the wrong place, you know? She always sort of regretted leaving him, I think." Sophia touched her finger to one of the amethyst earrings she'd always loved and sighed. "She gave me these when I was a girl. They'd been a gift from him. I think having them caused her more pain that she'd admit. Gram always said she didn't know what was worse—a love that was impossible or one that was practical and suitable. After what happened with Antoine, I think I realized that practical and suitable really isn't love at all. It was hard to understand at the time, but now I know that his infidelity broke my spirit, but it didn't break my heart."

"I'm glad he wasn't the great love of your life. You would have been far more hurt if it had been otherwise."

"Like you were?"

"What makes you say such a thing?" He conjured up a look so innocent Sophia couldn't help but chuckle.

"I get it. You won't talk about it. That's okay."

"I can't, that's all."

What was so awful he couldn't bring himself to talk about it? But then, Tomas wasn't the type to do much talking anyway. What little bits she got from him were too small to let her piece them together to get a complete picture. She traced a finger over the pink stone of the bridge. "Why is it parents—and grandparents, I suppose—think they know best?"

Disappointed by his silence, she pushed away from the bridge. "Well, at least you're not hiding a mistress somewhere." Suddenly her gaze narrowed. "Are you?"

He laughed, and relief flooded through her though she couldn't quite imagine why. "No," he chuckled, "I'm not hiding a mistress of any sort." He folded his arms. "Would it truly matter if I were?"

His soft question shattered the silence and she inhaled, held her breath. And then she turned her gaze up to him again and her chest constricted. "Yes," she murmured. "It would. It would destroy the good opinion I have of you, Tomas."

"Good opinion?" His mouth dropped open in surprise and then he shut it again just as quickly.

She wanted to tell him why but didn't know how without feeling like an idiot. How did she tell him what it meant for him to pay her the smallest compliment? How it restored her confidence when he wondered how Antoine could have let her get away? And the kiss aside, she had seen the worry and fear on his face as he'd leapt off his horse and come rushing to her side after she'd fallen off Neva. Yes, good opinion.

And to elaborate would make her look like a girl with a crush—starstruck by her knight in shining armor.

Sophia noticed a small girl standing on tiptoe a few meters away, her hands on the edge of the bridge. She swung her arm and two coins dropped into the water. When they sank to the bottom, the girl ran off, pigtails bobbing, to clasp her mother's hand and continue across the bridge.

"What's she doing?" Sophia asked, intrigued.

"Many people stand in this very spot and throw coins in the water," he said quietly. "They toss them in and make a wish."

Once again Sophia went to the edge and looked down. She wondered what the little girl had wished for. Tomas came up behind her. She felt his body close to hers, felt as though every place they nearly touched was alive. "What about you?" she asked quietly, trying to still the sensations coursing through her. "Have you made wishes?"

He pulled back, putting space between them and she sighed, shaking her hair back over her neck. Why was it she always seemed to ask the very thing that would break the spell?

She wondered how often he might have stood here in the past. She wondered what he had wished for. Did he believe in wishes at all? Or did he think this was just a tourist trap and a pretty story?

It took a while for him to answer, but when he did, his voice was low and rough from behind her. "I did, a long time ago."

"What did you wish for?"

Tomas sighed, and moved slowly to stand at the edge of the bridge, looking down into the water. "Things that could never be."

Sophia felt the same odd warning slide through her as she'd felt yesterday when he'd been so cryptic during their ride. Tomas was hiding something. He was so reticent, so closed-lipped, she knew it had to be big. She wanted to know, desperately. But what gave her the right to ask? They'd only known each other a few days. It was none of her business.

"Now you're going to chide me for holding out on you. For not baring my soul."

It was as if he read her mind. Sophia shook her head. "I know when I'm beaten. Getting anything out of you is like getting blood from a stone."

"Be careful what you wish for," he answered, dark tension clouding his voice.

"I haven't made a wish yet, so don't worry."

He dug into his pocket and drew out some coins, coming to stand beside her at the edge of the bridge. "Wishes should be happy things. They should be about looking forward." He held out his hand, offering her the change. "Didn't you come on this trip to look forward, Sophia?"

"Yes, I did."

"Then make your wish."

There it was, that swirling again, that anticipation of possibilities. His fingertips touched her palm as he gave her the money.

"I don't know what to wish for. It's been a wonderful day with you." She tilted her head up to look at him. "I've kind of enjoyed living in the moment."

"I've enjoyed it, too," he admitted. He raised an eyebrow. "Maybe you should wish for better riding skills. I'd like to take you out again this week."

"That might be a wise idea." She laughed lightly, but ended it on a soft sigh. "I needed this vacation badly," she murmured, watching a duck bobbing on the surface. "I didn't really know how much. Despite my obvious lack of equestrian prowess, I'm finding I kind of like myself. I haven't for a while."

Tomas leaned closer, putting his free hand on her waist. "You are turning out to be a surprise to me, too. You're not nearly as annoying as I thought you'd be."

Coming from Tomas, that was nearly a declaration. Her heart hammered at his nearness, and she felt herself get swept up in the moment. His lips hovered close and she rose up on her toes, tentatively touching her mouth to his.

The gentle contact blossomed into something more, something deeper, and Sophia clutched the coins tightly in her palm as her other hand gripped his arm. Behind them a group of boys hooted and clapped. She broke off the kiss, lowering her heels to the ground once more, slightly abashed and affected by the kiss just enough that she couldn't meet his gaze.

But that didn't stop Tomas from leaning forward and murmuring in her ear, "Make a wish, Sophia."

She closed her eyes, wished and tossed the coins into the shimmering water.

"Your turn," she said, turning away from the circles spiraling out from the coins she'd thrown.

Tomas shook his head. "No, I've made my wishes before. Today is for you to experience."

He looked so serious her heart stuttered and she smiled, trying to cajole him out of his somber mood. "Come on. What can it hurt? A few *centavos* in the river."

A dark look shadowed his features and Sophia drew back. "Tomas?"

He simply shook his head, stepping back, his face an immutable formation of angles and planes.

What had he wished for that had caused so much pain? She reached out and laid a hand on his arm. It was taut as a band of steel beneath her touch.

"What is it? Please, Tomas, tell me. Let me help you, like you've helped me."

"I should not have brought you here," he murmured. "You and your questions…"

"But you did bring me here, and it is lovely. There is more to you than you want people to see." She squeezed the muscle beneath her fingers. "But I see it. I know you are hurting. Does it have something to do with this bridge? Tell me what you wished for."

His dark gaze seared her for several seconds. "I wished to forget," he finally said, grinding out the words like shards of glass. "I wished to forget and now I wish to God I hadn't."

CHAPTER SIX

TOMAS wished he could bite back the words. What had made him admit such a thing? What was it about Sophia that got around his guard without him expecting it? Her kiss just now had nearly undone him. It had been innocent and sweet and freely given. She'd initiated it, not him. It hadn't been in anger or fear or any other sort of reactionary emotion, either. She had simply lifted her face like a rising sun and touched her lips to his.

He'd liked it—too much. So much that his mind had been wiped clean of anything but her until the boys had shouted and brought him crashing back to earth. He wasn't supposed to like it.

Dammit, she wasn't supposed to be able to see so much.

"Tomas." Her soft voice saying his name seemed to catch him right in the solar plexus, jamming up his breath. "What are you trying to forget? What has hurt you so much?"

He had to tell her. Had to tell someone or it would eat away at him like acid. He couldn't tell Maria or Carlos; he felt guilty enough already. With the changes going on at the estancia, it was as though the past was being erased a little more each day. With every new building and updated amenity he felt Rosa slipping further and further away. He knew Maria would not understand. She would be hurt, knowing he was moving on. And he wouldn't hurt Maria for the world.

"You are not the only one with a failed engagement, Sophia," he said quietly, running his fingers over the edge of the bridge. Sophia's lips dropped open and he clarified, "But it wasn't broken off. My fiancée died."

Sophia's large brown eyes glazed over with tears as she absorbed his words. "Oh, Tomas," she whispered. "That's horrible."

It had been. It had easily been the worst moment of his life, when the police had brought the news of Rosa's death. Like a knife to the heart, only the pain never went away.

"Was she ill?"

He shook his head. "No. She was mugged in Buenos Aires. The autopsy said the cause of death was blunt force to the head."

Sophia's fingers went to her mouth; he saw them trembling there. Her normally rosy cheeks drained of color. Why were the details so easy to repeat now? It was as though he was talking about another person, another lifetime. "It was three years ago," he finished.

"I'm so sorry," she murmured, taking his hands in hers. "And here I was whining over my situation. Oh Tomas," she whispered, her voice breaking, "How did you stand it?"

He spun away, away from the pity in her eyes and the sympathy in her voice. Turned away from the benevolent scene of ducks bobbing away on the water, evidence that the world kept on turning, blithely uninterested in whatever suffering he'd encountered. He had grieved so hard, so completely, that he would have done anything to take away the pain. "Now you know why I came to the bridge. There was a time that all I wanted to do was make the pain go away. To forget all the things that made me hurt."

"And you regret that now?"

He turned back and looked at Sophia, so young and naive. She really had no idea. "I shouldn't forget. I should be able to remember what she looked like, but sometimes I can't.

It's like she's there but blurred, you know? The sound of her voice when she laughed at a joke. The way she moved. Those things are slipping away from me." He scowled. "Especially when I'm with you."

"I make you forget?" Her voice was small.

"Yes, dammit, you do."

Long seconds passed and Tomas realized he'd been breathing fast and hard. He slowed his breaths to normal. He had made it sound as though this was her fault when it wasn't. "I'm sorry, Sophia. It is not your fault. It is mine."

"You don't need to grieve forever, Tomas. It is okay to move on. To have a life." She tried to curve her trembling lips into a smile, but they faltered. "To be happy. It doesn't mean you loved her less."

"Perhaps," he responded, knowing in his head she was right but feeling that heavy, sinking feeling in his heart just the same. "But it feels…"

"Disloyal to her memory?"

He nodded, not sure if he was relieved or not that she seemed to understand.

"Oh, Tomas. You are a good man beneath all your prickles and stings." Sophia took his hand and led him back to the edge of the bridge. He let himself be guided because he didn't know what else to do. "Is that why you hide away at the estancia?"

"At first it was to be close to her…"

Sophia's head whipped around to stare at him. Surprise widened her eyes and he realized that, of course, she didn't know the rest. "Rosa was Maria and Carlos's daughter," he clarified.

He saw the shock ripple across her face, and couldn't blame her. What would she say if she knew opening the estancia as a guest ranch had been his idea? Or if she knew he had been the financial backer behind it? He had already seen her impression of him change before his eyes as he told her about Rosa.

"I didn't see that coming," she admitted, and his eyes focused on her throat as she swallowed thickly. "So, what, you moved to the estancia after her death? To be close to her family?"

"They are *my* family, Sophia. Carlos and Maria are like parents to me. There was nowhere else I wanted to be. But since the fire, with all the changes happening, it doesn't feel the same. It is not the same place I came to when I was younger. I went home with Miguel and there she was. There they all were. I've been trying to hold on to that feeling, but it's slipping away."

"You're not just grieving for Rosa, then," Sophia replied softly. "You're grieving for everything that was and isn't anymore. You're grieving for your grief. And you feel awful for wanting to move on with your life. But Tomas....this is a good thing. Living now doesn't mean you didn't love her."

"It feels that way."

"But it won't bring her back. I know this is going to sound clichéd, but would she want you to go on hiding out at the estancia, never finding happiness again?"

The answer was simple. In theory.

"Why tell me, Tomas? Why now?"

Indeed. Yes, he'd been increasingly unsettled lately and the only people in the world he could really talk to were the last ones he should speak to about his feelings. "Because I can't talk to them. And you're here. And in a few days you'll be gone and it won't matter."

There was also the fact that there was this bizarre attraction to her, always simmering between them no matter what they were doing. She was bringing out all sorts of needs in him that he'd locked away for a long time. He pressed his lips together. That was more than he wanted her to know.

"I'm making it more difficult, aren't I?" Her cheeks

pinkened, a becoming flush of roses beneath her deep eyes. "I kissed you just now…"

How was it that she seemed to keep reading his thoughts? Having her put words to them fanned the flames all the more. "It's not your fault," he repeated. "You just make me…"

"Make you…?" the softly asked question came out with a wobble and he had the insane urge to wrap his arms around her.

"You make me want things," he admitted.

"Want me?" She lifted her chin boldly, but he could see through the gesture to the insecure girl behind it.

"Yes," he said, lifting his hand and placing it on her cheek. "Want you."

She looked down, biting her lip as if he'd flustered her. "I shouldn't have kissed you…"

He wanted to taste her lips so intensely again he knew it had to be a bad thing. "No, you shouldn't have."

"I'm not ready for a fling."

Of course she wasn't. She was on the heels of a broken engagement. He turned away, dropping his hand. "No. Sophia, I would never take advantage of you. Maybe that's why I told you. I don't want you to have any illusions of what is between us. Yesterday's kiss was a mistake."

"Of course."

The words sounded polite, but he detected a note of hurt behind them. "I didn't mean to make the afternoon so depressing," he said, needing to lighten the mood. This was why they needed to keep busy, occupied with other things!

"No, I'm glad you told me. It explains a lot. And I am sorry for your loss, Tomas. No one should have to endure such an ordeal."

"It is over and done," he replied. "I know it. I sometimes just have a problem being okay with it." He straightened his shoulders. "Now, let's shake off this heavy cloud and head back to the estancia."

He'd made some arrangements for while they were absent. The fact that the surprise excited him was a little worrying, but he shook it off. It didn't matter. It wouldn't matter. Sophia would be gone in a few days. Why shouldn't he enjoy her company until then?

Sophia's senses were whirling as she stood in the centre of her room, sorting through her purchases. Dinner was over and the mess tidied. Now the long evening stretched before her, leaving her too much time to think. Tomas had been engaged to Maria and Carlos's daughter. He had mentioned Miguel but not Rosa—a telling omission. And to have her taken in such a way…she suddenly realized there was a depth to Tomas that she hadn't counted on. For a man to close himself away from life as he had at the Vista del Cielo…beneath his tough exterior was a broken heart.

At first she had thought the swirling sensation she felt every time he was near was just physical. But, after today, she knew it was more. She felt a connection. And he felt it, too. He must, to trust her with such a confidence. How he must have grieved for the woman he loved. A woman who had grown up right here in this house, she realized. Of course letting go was hard when he was surrounded by reminders of her every day!

Sophia had just put her purchases away when Tomas showed up at her door. Simply seeing him there made her heart beat a little faster. Something had shifted between them. It had been daring of her to kiss him this afternoon. Maybe a simple kiss was not daring for some women, but it was for her. Taking the initiative was not her style, but there was something about Tomas that tempted her to try new things. She felt safe with him, a feeling she had never anticipated.

"Come with me. I want to show you something."

As his dark eyes watched her, an energy seemed to fill the room and she felt a little thrill. Following the set path had always been comfortable before, but she was beginning to see she'd been hiding behind it, too, the same way Tomas had hidden behind the estancia. Never taking risks. It was time for her to come out of the dark and find out just what Sophia Hollingsworth was made of.

Then there was the delicious tidbit that Tomas had admitted—he wanted her. She'd been honest—she wasn't ready for a fling, even though the thought was incredibly tempting. After this afternoon's shared honesty she felt she could trust him. He would not press her. And he was standing in the doorway looking like a kid on Christmas morning, impossible to resist.

"Okay, I'll play. Where are we going?"

"It's a surprise. Close your eyes."

A surprise? Tomas didn't seem the type for surprises. The heavy mood that had hung over them earlier had completely dissipated as his eyes danced at her. She closed her lids and felt him take her hand in his, leading her from her room and down the hall. With her eyes shut, she felt the intimacy of their connection running from her fingers straight to...well, straight to the part of her that kept insisting on being attracted to Tomas. It didn't help that every now and then this lighter side peeked from behind his rough exterior.

He led her out into the warm air, over prickly grass that tickled her legs and then she felt the dull hardness of patio stones beneath her feet.

"Open your eyes."

She lifted her lashes and squinted against the sun. Suddenly Sophia understood. They were at the pool. There was water in it, the reflection of the sun glimmering off the surface and filling the air with dancing light. "The pool!" she exclaimed, delighted. "You had it filled!"

"I had them come when we were gone. I wish you could enjoy it now, but I'm afraid it is too cold, and it needs time for the chemicals to balance. But I'll test it in the morning and you should be able to cool off and work on your back float tomorrow afternoon."

Sophia didn't know what to say. Of course this was part of the repairs Tomas had talked about but she got the feeling he had put a rush on it just for her. He clearly took pleasure in the surprise and the realization made her heart give a little skip. She took a step forward, could smell the sharp tang of chlorine and could feel the cool water on her skin even though it was just in anticipation. After all his bluster about the fire and repairs and lack of amenities, he had put a rush on the pool. To please her? Or to get her out of his hair? After what he'd told her on the bridge, Sophia wondered.

"Thank you, Tomas. For everything. For the day in town and for this great surprise."

"It had to be filled anyway," he replied. "You can enjoy it while I'm working."

Sophia couldn't help feeling a little deflated. Would it be so difficult for him to say a simple 'you're welcome?' Perhaps they'd broken through some barriers today, but it was clear that he wanted to get on with his work around the estancia now that she had the pool at her disposal.

"Yes, but it didn't need to be filled today. Tomorrow I'll help you with the chores and in the afternoon we'll go for a swim." She smiled her prettiest smile. She sensed that after this afternoon, he was trying to keep her at a distance. He would not get rid of her that easily. Tomas needed a bit of fun as much as she did. "It's no fun alone."

For a moment he hesitated, but she stuck out her hand to seal the bargain. Finally he took it, his big hand encompassing her smaller one until it all but disappeared within his fingers.

Tomas looked down at Sophia's glowing face and felt his heart do a little slide.

She had his number, no doubt about it. She'd seen through

his attempt to pass it off as no big deal. He had done it to please her and for that reason only—the arrangements had been made before this afternoon and what happened in town. "I thought it might help your hip," he said, pulling his hand away. "And any other sore muscles from the torture I'm putting you through."

She smiled up at him. He wished she'd stop doing that. She had a beautiful smile, easy and unaffected and it did funny things to him. Like today, on the bridge. What had he been thinking, kissing her back like that? Baring his soul?

"You are quite a taskmaster, but it's not torture," she teased. "I'm having fun. Truly."

"Right," he answered, and sent her a skeptical look.

She turned to look at the sparkling water. The flickering refraction of the sun on the surface lit her face, a shifting pattern of light and shadow that captivated him. "Whatever the reason, Tomas, it was awfully thoughtful. Thank you."

"Stop thanking me. If you remember correctly, you told me it should have been here waiting for your arrival."

Her cheeks coloured a little and an unfamiliar current seemed to heat him from the inside out. It was getting harder and harder to deflect her warmth and charm.

"Don't remind me, okay? I acted like a spoiled brat."

"I saw through that fairly quickly." Sophia had exhibited a fair bit of heart and willingness over the last few days, meeting each challenge he'd set out for her. He could add *beautiful* and *compassionate* to that list of qualities. It all combined to become a package to be reckoned with.

That he was even considering reckoning with her at all was shocking. He took a step back, a frown puzzling his brows. After hiding away for so long, the thought of consciously making a decision to move on was strange, even if he had been leading up to it for months. Now Sophia was insisting he join her in the pool tomorrow. He shouldn't, there was too much to do. There should not be any repeats of today's kisses or locked gazes, and the thought of her in a bathing suit, the cool water smooth against her skin…

He swallowed, trying to erase the image but failing utterly. Tomorrow night Maria and Carlos would return. The hours that he would have alone with Sophia were numbered, and he was surprised to find he didn't want them to end.

But what was the alternative? It would be wrong to let things go any further. She was a guest, he was the host. And there were things she still didn't know about him. Couldn't know, either. All she'd done since her arrival was stir things up. The more time they spent together, the more she seemed to sneak past his defences, and he had to put a stop to it.

Everything would settle again once Sophia went back to Canada. The estancia would be back in tip-top shape and they would go on as usual. The thought should have alleviated his worry, but it didn't. Because what he really wanted was more time with her.

And that was the most dangerous thing of all. The truth was she was cultivating feelings in him that scared him to death with their intensity.

"You knew I was afraid?" she asked, bending over and trailing her fingers in the water. He imagined the feel of her cool fingertips on his skin and swallowed.

"You covered it well. It was in the little things."

She nodded, making swirls with her fingers, random little shapes that rippled outward from her fingertips. "What things?"

"The look in your eyes. The way you tried to smile but didn't quite succeed."

Her fingers stopped moving. "I didn't realize I was so transparent."

Tomas went to her then, put his hand beneath her elbow and nudged until she stood beside him, the pool water dripping from her fingers. "Not your fault," he said quietly. "And you were right about some things. The estancia does have to hold a certain standard."

She smiled then, not a trace of fear or nervousness in her face. She was beautiful this way—unspoiled, artless. Irresistible.

"The estancia is perfect, Tomas, just as it is."

There it was, that burn that started deep within his belly every time she used that husky voice on him. Her acceptance of the estancia was simply another thread weaving their connection together.

He wanted more. It shocked him how much more. She had plagued his thoughts ever since they'd kissed in the yard. It hadn't just been anger that had driven him to take her in his arms. It had also been fear and need and desire. Emotions he'd locked away long ago, determined not to feel them again.

The banked fire in her eyes only fed the flames of desire burning through him. There was a flush to her cheeks that was caused by more than the sun beating down on them, and her eyes shone up at him. It suddenly seemed like too much work to carry on fighting against the attraction that kept flaring up like a hotspot that refused to go out. Forget what if and the past. It was over and done. What if he took her in his arms right now? What would happen then?

His gaze dropped to her lips. "You need to be careful when you look at me that way."

Her lashes fluttered as he leaned closer. He knew what he wanted. The same thing he'd wanted ever since he'd kissed her on the bridge. He wanted to lose himself in her, just for a little while. To live again, as he hadn't lived in three years. It had been his choice. Always his choice. But Sophia had awakened something in him. Curiosity. And hunger. He wanted more.

She tried to hide it, but he knew she was just as curious about him as he was about her. It was in the sidelong glances, the way she pulled back from the little touches as though his skin was on fire. The way her lips tasted. The little sound she made as their kiss ended. Was she even aware she did that? Did she know how hard it was for him to walk away? He wasn't sure he could any longer.

He watched, fascinated, as her tongue sneaked out to wet her lips. She was nervous. Somehow the thought was comforting. He was glad she wasn't taking this attraction—if that was what it could be called—in stride. He wasn't completely insensitive to what she'd been through. She'd caught her fiancé with another woman, for heaven's sake. She'd come on her honeymoon alone. A deliberate act of defiance, but he could see through it to the insecurity underneath. He adored her for it.

They were only a breath apart. "You, Sophia, are a delightful contradiction."

"What sort of contradiction?"

Her lids fluttered open and he could see the reflection of himself in her pupils. Had he ever needed a woman with such intensity? He cupped her face in his hands, gathering strength from feeling her soft skin against his palms, finally giving in to the insane desire he'd been feeling ever since she'd arrived and making the conscious decision to let it have its way. "One side gutsy and brilliant. The other side fragile as a flower. Both sides equally attractive, you see. *Querida,* there are times I'm not quite sure what to do with you."

"*Querida...*" she murmured, their lips only inches apart, "What does that mean?"

His heart clubbed, hearing her say the Spanish word, wanting to hear her say it again. "It means *darling,*" he replied, and the simple voicing of the sentiment ratcheted everything up another notch. Darling. Was she his? Or was he hers? Did it matter?

She lifted her hand and put it over top of his, then turned her head to kiss his palm. "*Querida*," she murmured thoughtfully. "Tell me, which side do you like most?"

Her voice was soft, but it shook, and Tomas knew he was sunk.

"This one," he replied, and lowered his mouth.

CHAPTER SEVEN

SOPHIA melted against him. *Finally.* Her body seemed to breathe the sentiment as she returned the kiss, looping her arms around his neck and losing her fingers in his hair. Her heart accelerated as she let herself give in to the moment, realizing where she was and who she was with and just awed enough to be stunned by it all. She felt like a butterfly set free from a cocoon. No longer the Sophia of old, but a reinvented one, seeing new places, trying new things. And one of those things was a very sexy Argentinian willingly in her arms.

The kiss gentled and Tomas pulled his lips away from hers, though they hovered near her ear and his breath sent shivers down her spine. His hands rested on her hips. Suggestion slid through the air and Sophia felt all her nerve endings kick into overdrive. She ran her hands down his shoulder blades, marveling at the taut muscles beneath the cotton of his shirt.

And then he touched his lips to the soft spot behind her ear and whatever else was in her mind fled.

The early evening sun sent a blaze of amber light across the yard as Tomas slid his mouth across her cheek and captured her lips again. He pulled her against him with a new urgency and the air caught in her lungs.

"Tomas, I…" She wanted to find the words but somehow couldn't string them together. How could she explain how much she wanted him? How touched she'd been that he'd confided in her this afternoon, and how awed she was that he wasn't pushing her as she'd expected? How could she resist a man who had loved so deeply? She knew perhaps she should be careful. He was moving on but reluctantly so. It was potentially a red flag, but as his hands spanned her waist she knew that the depth of his feeling for Rosa was part of his allure. He was touching her so gently, so reverently, that she was afraid she'd melt into a pool at his feet.

How could she explain how special he was and then express her own hesitation and fear? Why did she keep holding back? She was twenty-five years old and an independent woman. Why did it have to be so difficult to make the choice to move forward?

She sighed with bliss as his lips touched the underside of her jaw, the curve of her neck. His hand trailed over her hip to cup her bottom.

She knew why she held back. She was smart enough to know that the way they were holding each other—touching each other—created a certain expectation. It was foreplay. It wasn't that she didn't want him. She did. She closed her eyes and knew she shouldn't let her inexperience matter so much. What was she waiting for? Tomas would be gentle and… Her body shivered with pleasure as his fingers played in her hair. And thorough. A gasp erupted from her lips as he licked the column of her neck.

But Tomas wasn't expecting a virgin.

Gently he cupped her jaw with his hand. "Are you sure, Sophia?"

Of course she wasn't. Everything her body was screaming right now was at war with her heart and head. Making love for the first time was important. She wanted it to go right. She didn't want to be awkward or show her inexperience. She wanted it to be with the right person. As she looked up into his eyes, her heart thumped. She knew he was a good man.

His actions had shown it and this afternoon had confirmed it. But she wasn't able to form an answer to his question.

Tomas didn't wait. "Sophia," he murmured, and did what every woman fantasized about at least once in their lives— he scooped her up in his arms. The first time he'd done this, after her fall, had been a surprise. This time it was filled with a darker intention, and it thrilled her right to her toes.

With strong, purposeful strides he carried her to the door of the house and into the cool, shadowed hallway. She looped her arms around his neck and pressed her lips to the side of his throat, tasting his warm and slightly salty skin. She could do this. She could. She *wanted* to. Here, on the wild plains of South America, with the warm, scented wind wafting through the windows, carrying the sweet sound of the finches in the bushes outside. Here nothing else mattered. Just Tomas. And her. Two damaged souls healing each other.

He took her to the room he occupied in the family quarters at the opposite end of the house. It was smaller than her room, and hadn't been through the obvious renovation of the guest wing. But it was warm, with woven mats covering the floor and a homemade blanket stretched out on the bed. The window was open, the draft tingling over her skin as Tomas laid her carefully on top of the blanket.

And, oh, he was so gentle. Instead of using his physicality to dominate, he shattered her with patience, opening up all her nerve endings and making her feel beautiful, desirable beneath his touch.

He took his time, removing the clip from her hair, letting the weight of it fall around her shoulders. He sank his fingers in it and Sophia closed her eyes, luxuriating in the feel of his hands against her scalp.

"I love your hair," he said roughly, tightening his fingers so that he controlled her head. He lifted and brought her face up to his. "The colour of flames," he said. "The colour of sunset on the pampas."

Then he was kissing her again. It was heavenly, and a bit surreal knowing he couldn't seem to help himself. She moved against him, feeling the warmth of his skin through her shirt.

She was in danger of losing herself completely as he disentangled his hands from her curls and made short work of her light blouse. Trepidation vibrated inside her, but she pushed it away. She wanted this. She trusted him. It wasn't until he reached for the button of her jeans that she couldn't breathe and instinctively put a hand down to stop him.

"Tomas..."

"Too fast?" His breath was laboured now and the room seemed full of his heartbeat as she pressed her palm to his chest.

"It's not that, it's..."

But how could she tell him? She felt the heat rush to her face. What would he think of her? She already felt awkward and like a teenager trapped in a woman's body. And Tomas was such a strong force, so much larger than life. He'd suffered so much. She was awestruck by him and felt so completely out of her league.

"What is it, *querida?*"

He was calling her darling again and it made her heart want to weep. He was still holding her, but his brows had drawn together and she now felt utterly silly seeing the concern darkening his eyes. She felt a sting behind her nose and the ridiculous urge to curl up in his embrace to make everything right.

"Sophia?" He put a finger under her chin and lifted it, forcing her to look into his eyes. Why couldn't this be carefree and easy? Why was it so hard to let go of the past and step forward into a new, reinvented Sophia? Instead she felt nothing but mortified. And the caring way he was looking at her now told her he deserved an explanation. No, not just an explanation. The truth. Nothing but the truth would be right for Tomas. Not after today.

"Whatever it is, you can tell me."

"I have never…I mean…"

He chuckled, the lines clearing from his face in relief. "Sophia, I wouldn't think as much of you if you did this all the time. I cannot deny I feel a connection to you that is very unexpected. When you first arrived…" He paused, shook his head. "I have hidden myself away for a long time, Sophia. You know that."

Oh God. He thought her reservations were about having a one-night stand? Once more she felt unbearably young and naive.

If only it were as simple as a one-nighter. If that were her biggest obstacle, she'd not stand a hope of coming through this with her dignity intact. But she had to tell him. It wasn't as if he wouldn't find out… Her breath caught as she realized exactly what would happen.

"No," she stopped his hand, which was reassuringly stroking her shoulder. "Tomas please…" the words came out all strangled and she fought her way through them "…I've never done *this* before."

"This…" There were the wrinkles again as he sat back, clearly confused. "You mean…"

"*This*," she replied meaningfully. "Any of it."

"You're a…"

"Yes," she said, her voice finally coming out strong and clear. "I am." And the little voice inside her had to know. "Does it make a difference?"

He reached out for her hands. "Matter? Of course it matters! Sophia, you must be…"

"Twenty-five," she offered, wincing inside as the words came out a bit primly. She squared her shoulders. "I am twenty-five years old and I have never had sex. There. I said it."

The smile he sent her way was soft and indulgent. "I had been going to say afraid."

She wanted to sink through the floor.

She *was* scared. She had built this moment up in her mind for so long that when suddenly faced with it she turned coward, unable to go through with it. What if she didn't know what to do? Tomas might be patient but how far would his patience extend? It was easier to back away.

"Not even with your fiancé?" he probed gently.

It would have been better if he had been repulsed by her admission. That would have been much easier than the way his gentleness seemed to hold a mirror up to her flaws. She'd put her faith in the wrong things, and now had to admit to herself that she had been played for a fool, convincing herself Antoine had loved her enough to wait.

But that was the problem. He hadn't loved her, and deep down she'd known it. She had struggled for Antoine's approval just as she had from everyone else in her life, too, and she'd never quite gotten it. He'd been remarkably patient about not having sex. But she understood now. It was because he hadn't wanted to. He hadn't wanted *her*. He'd had his mistress for sex.

And now Tomas was here, and he wanted her, and knowing it was beautiful. And yet she was still too afraid.

Afraid that she'd get in too deep and end up hurt in the end. Because Tomas was temporary. It wasn't even a question of *when* he would take his love away. It wasn't hers to begin with. He might be ready to move on and leave his grief behind, but it was a long leap from there to love. And as much as she'd like to think she was modern enough to disassociate sex from love, she just couldn't.

She shook her head in answer to Tomas's question and already she could feel the distance opening up between them. It was clear the moment was over. Being swept away in the magic only went so far, and she had no one to blame but herself. She'd made a calculated risk, overestimated herself and failed. Again.

She pushed herself back on the bed and began rebuttoning her blouse. Once it was fastened she pulled her knees toward her chest and hugged them with her arms. Tomas sat down at the opposite end, his back against the iron foot rail. To her surprise he reached out and put a warm hand on her ankle, tethering them together, reassuring.

"The more you speak of this Antoine, the more I am convinced he's a total fool," Tomas said quietly, his thumb rubbing persistent circles around her ankle bone.

"He didn't love me, and that's the end of it," she replied, but she couldn't help feeling a little empty. "He never did. And I wouldn't want him back now for any reason." She looked up at Tomas, who was watching her patiently. "But it might have been nice to know that maybe he did love me, once."

"Sex isn't always about love, you know."

He gave a small smile, and his eyes twinkled at her just a little bit. She adored the way he was looking at her, appreciated how he was trying to make things right again, but she couldn't quite manage to get there. "But don't you think it should be?"

His thumb paused. "Obviously you do." Then it started circling again. "Sophia Hollingsworth, you are incredibly old-fashioned despite first impressions."

"I'm sorry…"

"It wasn't a criticism."

The whole conversation, rather than putting her off, was making her appreciate Tomas's good qualities all the more and that was a frightening idea. She craved the intimacy, but it terrified her as well.

She was a mess, she realized. And she had been for some time.

"I don't want to be in love," she admitted, and the silence

in the room was momentarily deafening. "And I know you don't, either."

The evening waned and the shadows lengthened in the room. Tomas shifted to the head of the bed and put his arm around her, pulling until she turned into the curve of his arm. She thought of the way he'd picked her up in his arms and a curl went through her tummy. Why did he have to be so damned honorable?

"You're right," he murmured. "I don't want to be in love. But I like you, Sophia. I like you a lot."

"I am afraid of spiders and can't ride a horse."

"Well, there is that."

She rested her cheek on his shoulder.

"I'm not really good at anything."

"You are good at trying. I respect that, Sophia."

She wanted to ask him if he could ever see himself being in love again, but she kept the words buttoned up inside. The night had been embarrassing enough without bringing the topic of Rosa into it. She knew she should push away and go to her own room. The very thought made her so lonely her chest cramped. Tomas on one side of the house, her on the other. She was tired of being alone. She was tired of having to pretend she was strong. She had spent years following the rules, doing what was asked of her because she'd been afraid of being alone. Afraid of having that love taken away should she make a mistake.

Well, here she was, in spite of her best efforts, alone anyway. Except for Tomas. And he was making her see that toeing the line was no guarantee. From now on she wanted to be herself. And those that loved her would love her for that—not because she'd done what they wanted.

But oh, it was hard to let go. The backs of her eyes burned with unshed tears.

"I should go," she whispered, knowing that if she were going to cry it would be better to do it privately.

* * *

Tomas knew he should let her go. He could hear the tears in her voice and he knew he should be running in the other direction. Slaking his need for her was one thing. Taking a virgin was another—especially one who felt that making love actually should have some ingredient of love in it. He closed his eyes, knowing he'd gotten himself in too deep.

The problem was that he knew she was right. When two people shared bodies, hearts got involved, and his relationship with her—could it be called a relationship?—was complicated enough. Making love to her now was out of the question. But sending her off to her own room felt callous and cold. Instead Tomas shifted his weight and lifted the blanket, covering them both as they slid down the bed.

"Don't go yet. I don't want you to leave upset."

"I'm not." And still she held on to his warmth and he felt her soft curves curl against him. He tightened his arm. It felt so natural, so right.

"Let me hold you for a while, then."

She let out a breathy sigh and her head relaxed fully against the curve of his shoulder. Tomas felt something open up inside him. It had been so very long since he'd held a woman this way. Since he'd let someone trust him—since he'd trusted himself. Sophia made him feel good and strong. Protective and invincible.

Which should have been a wonderful, beautiful thing.

But as her breath evened out and she fell asleep, her breath moist on his skin, all he felt was regret, sharp and bittersweet.

The sun filtered in through the window as Sophia woke, the corners of her eyes gritty with sleep. She was curled up next to Tomas's body, her head tucked beneath his chin and her ear pressed against his warm chest. She could just make out his heartbeat and the rise and fall of his steady breathing. She closed her eyes again, indulging in the moment of being held in his arms while he slept. Her cheeks burned as she realized that she had managed to do something she had never done before. She had spent the night in a man's arms. In Tomas's arms. They had slept together in the most literal sense of the term.

For that, she most definitely was not sorry.

She opened her eyes again and very carefully shifted so she could rest on her elbow and examine him. She got a thrill simply looking at him sleeping: his golden skin so much darker than her own pale, slightly freckled complexion, the thick fringe of lashes that lay on his cheeks and the hint of dark stubble on his jaw. For a fleeting moment she let herself believe that he was hers. No one else's. Just hers. It was an unsettling feeling knowing she wanted him to be. Sex or not, her feelings for Tomas were growing and becoming more complicated. Not love, but definitely something.

She counted down days. Only three left, after today. Her time here was drawing short, and she found she didn't want to go home yet, even though she knew she must. It was more than the country working on her heart, she realized. More than the novelty and the exoticism of it, so very different from her own way of life. More than the comfort and peace of the estancia. No, it was Tomas. She knew that months from now when she looked back, it would be Tomas she would remember most. Tomas whose face would still be clear in her mind.

Her hand began to fall asleep and she carefully tried to change position. Tomas's lashes flickered and then raised. When the sleep cleared, his eyes focused on her, and she felt the queer lifting in her chest once again. Tomas tightened his arm around her and pulled her in against him, drawing her close and dropping a light kiss on her forehead.

"*Buenos dias,*" he said softly, and Sophia smiled against him, feeling that any errors of the previous night were forgiven.

"*Buenos dias* to you, too," she replied. She supposed now

that they were both awake they'd have to get up and out of their cozy cocoon. But Tomas's possessive arm stayed where it was and she held on awhile longer.

"The bed is too comfortable," he grumbled. "I suppose I should get up and tend to the animals." Tomas shifted on to his side so he was facing her. "You could help me today. You can wear your new jeans and you can help me move the cattle."

"You'd trust me to do that?" She rose up on to her elbow. Were they not going to speak of last night then? On one hand she was vastly relieved, and she was pleased he had asked her to help today. But on the other, it showed her nothing had changed for him. It was back to work as usual.

"Of course. It will be fun. It is one of the things Carlos will be doing with tourists, you know. I'll show you what to do. And I would like your company."

"I'd like to go with you," she admitted. What had she expected? Morning declarations and flowery speeches? Of course not. She would show him that nothing had changed for her, either. "It would be lonely here in the house alone."

"Maria and Carlos will be back this evening. It won't be quiet for long."

When she'd first arrived Sophia had wished for the Rodriguezes' presence simply so she wouldn't have to butt heads with Tomas. Now she wanted more time alone with him, and he sounded relieved that Maria and Carlos would be here to run interference. Sophia suddenly felt embarrassed about last night, clinging to him when she should have gone to her own room. He'd only been polite. He'd acted kindly instead of pushing her away. She wanted to bury her face in her hands, but resisted. Now she just wanted to get out of here.

"Sophia…"

"Hmm?" She sat up and began to swing her legs over the edge of the mattress.

"I want to apologize for how I treated you when you arrived."

The apology gave her pause and she carefully put her feet on the floor. She forced a laugh and looked over her shoulder at him. "I deserved it. I might not be very good at this ranch stuff, Tomas, but I think I am done with putting on appearances. It feels liberating, so don't apologize."

She pushed herself up off the bed and ran her hands down her wrinkled blouse. "Now, if we're going to be working today, we need a good breakfast. I'm going to make pancakes."

He raised an eyebrow. "Are you now?"

"Yes, I am. You're not the only one who can cook, you know." He wasn't the only one who could do a lot of things. Like pretend last night never happened.

"Have you been holding out on me, Señorita Hollingsworth?" He pushed himself to a sitting position and she tried not to stare at the bare expanse of his chest, and the warm skin where, up until a few minutes ago, she'd been snuggling.

His teasing was light with innuendo, and she couldn't help the bit of relief that rushed through her as she replied, "Most definitely, Señor Mendoza."

"Then get to it. After lunch, we can try out the pool."

Sophia's cheeks warmed as she scuttled from Tomas's bedroom. So he would come with her after all. She told herself not to get her hopes up, not to read more into things than was there. Last night had been a disaster and this morning there hadn't even been a good morning kiss. No, there was nothing more going on with her and Tomas.

Nevertheless, the thought of basking in the sun with him, dressed only in her two-piece suit gave her a queer feeling in her stomach.

Sophia finished the tidying while Tomas got the horses. She quickly changed, deciding on her new jeans for a morning spent in the saddle, as well as a cotton shirt, boots and the dusty *campero* she'd worn during her first eventful ride. As she passed by the living room, her gaze fell once more on the girl in the photo. She was still smiling, so confident as she sat on her horse. She frowned as a sudden thought occurred. Was this Rosa? Sophia's cheeks flamed. It very well could be. The face was happy and carefree, the picture taken just outside the barn here at the estancia—Sophia could see the door on the edge of the photo. It gave her an odd feeling, knowing she'd been in Rosa's house, sharing a bed with Tomas. As if she were trespassing somehow.

It was better that they hadn't gone through with it last night, she realized. Nothing could come of their relationship. All she could worry about was the here and now. Today, Sophia would help Tomas. Today, she would refuse to let anything else matter.

Tomas had the horses ready and Sophia let the maudlin thoughts flutter away on the dry wind as together they worked their way south. He showed her how to position her mount to urge the cattle in a specific direction, and other than calling his instructions, the distance between them prevented any real conversation. But Sophia didn't mind. She was actually having fun. Moving the cattle and working the horse took all her physical and mental concentration. She'd be tired later, but for now it was invigorating.

She reined to the left and brought several cows back into the group as Tomas shouted his approval. She urged the last one through the gate and took off her hat, swinging it through the air in victory. Tomas dismounted, moving to close the latch.

"I told you you could do it," he said, dusting off his hands and squinting up at her.

"It is not a very large herd," she acknowledged, but inside she was proud of her achievement. If someone had told her even a week ago she'd be herding cattle, she'd have laughed in their face. Now here she was, dusty, dirty, hot and happy. She dusted off the *campero* and put it back on her head.

"It doesn't matter. There were only two of us and it worked."

"I think I stopped needing to prove something," she admitted. "And I just wanted to help."

"Well, you did a fine job for a beginner. Are you sure you don't want a job as a hand here?"

He was joking but the idea temporarily knocked Sophia off her pins. For a split second she thought about leaving her whole life in Canada behind and making a complete change. It was a giddy thought. But she dismissed it as quickly as it had come. It was also silly. She was no ranch hand, and she didn't belong here. He was just teasing.

"You're very funny, Tomas. And you know once Carlos is back you'll have everything handled."

Tomas held up a hand, halting any more discussion.

"What is it?" She looked around, wondering if he'd heard some animal she wasn't aware existed in this part of the world. His eyes were sharp and his cheekbones taut as he scanned the pasture. "Are we in danger?"

"Sophia. For God's sake, hush," he commanded.

He looked at the retreating herd and she saw his lips move as if he were counting. "It is as I thought. We're short one. Are you sure you didn't miss any?"

Great. Had she messed up again?

"You take the far side, and I'll come up this way. If you find our missing cow, call out."

Sophia nudged her mare towards the far side of the pasture. Why had her first thought been that of failure? Of doing something wrong? A fly buzzed around her head and she swatted at it, annoyed. She was far too desperate for his approval. Why did she continue letting him be so important?

Because he was the one person who challenged her, and seemed to think she could meet the challenges he put before her. He wasn't setting her up to fail. He pushed. She was learning to push back. And dammit, she was learning to respect him, too. It would be easier to resent his perfect hide if she didn't.

Tomas called out; Sophia had half hoped she'd be the one to find the stray animal just to prove a point. Instead she slowly made her way across the field to where Tomas was already examining the errant cow.

"She's cut," he said, examining the leg below the knee joint. "I don't have my bag with me..."

Sophia interrupted him with a raised brows. "You mean you're not prepared?"

"Not this time. We'll have to ride back, and I'll come back out with supplies. It's not bad, but there's always concern of infection."

They rode back to the barn, Sophia managing an easy canter behind Tomas. When they rode into the barnyard, Sophia looked over at him. "Do you need help? I can come with you."

"No, I'll be fine. Let's just turn Neva out for some fresh grass."

Sophia helped him remove the saddle and bridle from Neva and she turned the mare out into the paddock by herself, a task she could never have accomplished a few days ago.

"Go enjoy a swim," he said as he began packing things into a leather bag, but he paused to squeeze her hand. "I don't know how long I'll be, and you should enjoy the afternoon. I'm sorry I can't join you, Sophia."

She couldn't quite erase the feeling that he was conveniently out of her path for the afternoon. But the incident was also a clear reminder to Sophia that this was a working ranch, and that Tomas's job also included caring for the stock in addition to interacting with guests. And this week he'd been doing the jobs of four people—cook and host, handyman and gaucho. He looked weary as he mounted his horse again, but she smiled. "I will. I'll see you later."

The pool was gloriously cool, but after a half hour Sophia got out and spent a few moments basking in the sun. It was only early afternoon and she didn't know when Tomas would be back, and even though he could be completely exasperating, the day seemed empty without his company. Carlos and Maria were returning and she knew Tomas had wanted to finish several jobs before their arrival. A new energy filled her as an idea blossomed. She knew Tomas expected her to soak up an afternoon of leisure. It was what he'd *told* her to do. But Sophia was quite enjoying exercising her own mind, and he would be in for a surprise when he returned if she had anything to say about it.

As the golden orb of the sun sank towards the horizon, Sophia made her last swipe with the brush, put it across the top of the can, and braced her hands against her lower back, easing out the ache.

Then a dot appeared on the horizon where the pampas met the sky and Sophia felt her heart thump. For a few moments she watched as it got gradually bigger, until she could see that it was horse and man. He was cantering across the plain, straight and tall in the saddle, and Sophia forgot her aching muscles and jogged to the gate. As she opened it, she heard the hoofbeats match the motion of the stride and she swung the gate wide to let them through.

The look of surprise on Tomas's face as he slowed and trotted through the gap was worth all the hard work she'd put in.

She closed and latched the gate behind him and followed him to the barn. He dismounted, leading the gelding through and cross-tying him to remove the tack. Sophia hung back, simply watching the way Tomas's muscles moved beneath his shirt as he removed saddle and pad.

But when the saddle was put away, the horse watered and turned out, Tomas put his hands on his hips and looked her up and down.

"And what have you been up to? Because that doesn't look like the swimsuit I imagined you'd wear for an afternoon poolside."

First of all, the idea that he'd imagined her in a bathing suit sent a tingle through her body. Then she realized she was in the dirty coveralls again. And that she had yet to clean up the mess from the painting. Brush and can still sat beside the shed door.

"I have a surprise for you," she said, excited to show him her handiwork.

She led him to the shed and watched his face as he saw the fresh paint. "You did this?"

She nodded. "I knew you wanted to have it done for Maria and Carlos's return."

Her excitement turned sour when the smile slipped from his face and his jaw tightened. "What is it? Did I do something wrong? Is the job not good enough?"

"You didn't have to do this," he said sharply. "You should have spent the afternoon by the pool."

All her elation sank into a pit of disappointment. She'd wanted to please him. She'd wanted to help, to pay him back for the things he'd done for her all week. The low feeling was suddenly infused with anger. At him, for taking the pleasure of completing the task away from her and at herself, for letting him. She stalked over to the can and brush and picked both up. She spun back, intending to head to the barn but he shot out a hand, stopping her—and paint splashed up over the lid and down the leg of the coveralls.

Oh-so-coolly, Sophia reached out and removed his hand from her arm.

"I did go for a swim," she informed him. "It was lovely. And I felt absolutely useless. So I decided to finish what we started the other day. You would have, if you'd had time. And I knew you wanted it done for Maria and Carlos's return. So yes, I did it. Not that you're grateful in any way, shape or form."

Tomas pulled off his hat and ran his hand through his hair, leaving the curls lying in rills on his head. A smudge of dirt darkened his cheek and Sophia inhaled, fortifying herself. It was not sexy. It was not.

And perhaps if she told herself that long enough, she might just believe it.

She swept past him, determined to clean the brush and put the lid back on the can before going to the house. She was glad the Rodriguezes would be back tonight! Maybe she'd have someone to talk to who didn't feel the need to move between both ends of an emotional barometer!

"Sophia!" His steps sounded behind her, boots on hard ground. She refused to turn around, just kept walking, bound up in righteousness and feeling vastly unappreciated.

"Sophia! Wait."

She stopped at the imperious command, then with a toss of her head started off again.

He refused to chase after her. "You are so infuriating!" he called.

That had her turning around. "So are you!"

He'd meant it when he'd said he didn't know what to do with her. He'd phrased it all wrong, he knew. But any other words he formed in his head seemed to say way more than he wanted to. If things hadn't halted last night, he knew he would have made love to her. Just the thought of it now was enough to tie him in knots. And it would have been a huge mistake. Now it seemed everything he'd said made her angrier with him. Was it what he said or was it because of last night?

He'd be damned if he'd ask her.

"I just meant…you're a guest, Sophia. This wasn't necessary."

"This is a working estancia, right? Didn't you tell me that one of the big draws is helping out?"

"Well, yes, but…"

"But I didn't do the job well enough? Is that it?"

"No, it looks great, but…"

"But what?"

Tomas took a step forward, his patience wearing thin. It had been a long, hot afternoon and he'd tried putting her out of his mind and could not to his growing irritation. "If you would let me get a word in, I would tell you that I did not expect you to do this. This is above and beyond. It is my responsibility to have things repaired, not yours."

"Is that your version of thank you?"

How he could want to kiss and throttle a woman at the same time was beyond him.

"I do thank you." The shed did look wonderful. And Sophia was riled up and looking as gorgeous as he'd ever seen her, even in the ratty coveralls. "It's not that. I put that expectation on you and I shouldn't have."

"And so the painting on the first day? That wasn't my job, either?"

She had him there. She knew exactly why he'd had her painting the first day. She'd come in with her fancy shoes and the chip on her shoulder and he'd wanted to teach her a lesson. "I was testing you, all right? Pushing you. Which, by the way, I have already apologized for. I thought we'd moved past this."

She lifted a finger and shook it. "And yet today what did you do? Came back issuing edicts on what I should and should not do. I have my own mind, Tomas Mendoza. So you can take your imperatives and…and…"

"Stuff them?"

A smile made its way to her mouth, though she tried not

to show it. Her lips twitched as she admitted, "Those weren't quite the words I was thinking of."

"You shook your finger at me just the way Maria does. There may be hope for you yet."

"Why do we always fight?"

"We don't...always."

He shouldn't have said it. Her mouth opened and closed a few times and he knew they were both thinking about the other thing they seemed to do with disturbing regularity—kiss.

She put her hand in the pocket of her coveralls. "You were busy doing other things today," she said finally. "Your work and Carlos's and Maria's. And getting pools filled and taking me to town. So pardon me for trying to help."

He sighed, so heavily it felt like the weight of the world was on his shoulders. And bit by bit the anger fuelling him drained away.

"It was meant as a gift, Tomas. Nothing more. A chance for me to help you. Don't you think I've noticed how hard you work?"

"And I thank you for the gift, Sophia, I do. But I feel guilty about it just the same."

"Why?"

"Because..." He came forward and took the paint can and brush from her hands. "Because finishing the shed was my job, not yours. You were right. This is your vacation, it's not slave labour. And I would have had it done if..."

"If?"

"If I hadn't been enjoying myself with you."

The boutique wasn't restocked and he'd left the second coat of paint to spend the day in town with Sophia instead. He'd managed to get the pool filled, but with the work crew not coming until the weekend to work on the spa building... He should have had it all done. He knew how Maria felt about the damage, how nervous the fire had made her. That should have been his priority. Not kissing and making wishes on bridges and...

And every other thing that had been on his mind today. Moving on for real, not just in his head.

"Can we stop yelling now?" she asked.

"Yelling is safer," Tomas said, going to the sink and running water for the brush.

"Safer than what?"

His hands paused under the water and Sophia's mouth formed a knowing O.

He gave up and put the brush to soak, turning off the water.

"I do appreciate the work on the shed, more than you know," Tomas offered. "And so will Carlos and Maria. Maria especially. The fire hit her hard, Sophia. It frightened her. She wanted things back the way they were, and I wanted most of the work to be done because of that. The estancia is starting to look even better than it did before. But I feel awful that I made you think you needed to do this."

"You didn't make me do anything. I was sitting by the pool, bored, wondering what you were doing, and I took the idea to do it." She lifted her gaze to his, a challenge but with that bit of shyness that hit him in the gut every single time. "I wanted to do it. For you."

For him? The notion took the starch out of his argument, leaving him floundering. Oh God, the last thing he needed was Sophia getting serious romantic notions about him. They couldn't get in too deep. And yet he couldn't find it in himself to push her away, or be sorry. There was something in her gaze now, something he hadn't seen before, and it changed the air between them. It was like the loosening of a screw, the untying of a knot, and taking off the pressure made him feel more trapped, rather than less.

He'd thought last night was the closest he'd ever be to her, and that was the safest course. But he'd been wrong. Right now they were connected in a way he'd never felt before, and he didn't even know why.

"Maria and Carlos will arrive soon," he said finally. To explore what was going on between them would be a mistake. Sure, maybe Sophia had brought him out of his well-guarded shell, and maybe he was having fun. Was it so wrong to enjoy a few precious days? She'd be gone soon enough and he'd still be here at Vista del Cielo.

"You should go get cleaned up. I'll look after this."

It was all she was going to get from him. As she turned her back on him he knew this was the last time they'd be this alone. Any moment would mark the return of Maria and Carlos. And after that, it was back to Canada for Sophia.

CHAPTER EIGHT

WHEN Sophia emerged from her room in fresh jeans and a T-shirt, Maria and Carlos had arrived. Sophia stepped into the kitchen amid the chatter and stood shyly, not sure how to interrupt. A small, dark-haired woman was shaking a finger at Tomas and Tomas was laughing at her. A man—Carlos— was watching with a smile on his face. He saw Sophia first and smiled at her.

"You must be Sophia. I am Carlos, and this is Maria. Welcome to Vista del Cielo, though our welcome is long overdue."

Maria spun around, a ball of energy that filled the room with light. She rattled off a greeting in enthusiastic Spanish— the words were lost on Sophia but not the meaning. Barely over five feet, she was a firecracker. "We're so glad you could join us, Sophia. And first thing tomorrow we will straighten out your reservation, I promise." Then she came forward and gave Sophia a welcoming hug and beamed.

The reservation. Sophia had forgotten all about it! "Don't worry about it. If it was a mix-up, it's been a most pleasur-able one." She looked at Tomas as she said the last, feeling a little challenge build. She knew that Tomas would never want Maria to know how they'd fought—and how they'd made up, too. She smiled, wondering if she'd finally found his weak spot in the woman who would have been his mother-in-law.

"And our Tomas has been a good host." It was a statement from Maria, not a question. Sophia nearly laughed. Yes, it gave her a perverse pleasure speaking to Maria while Tomas waited in the background. She wondered what Maria would say if she knew about falling off the horse. Or that Sophia had painted the shed. Or that she had kissed 'our Tomas' on the *Puente Viejo* just before making a wish.

"The very best," she replied, sobering. This was also Rosa's mother, the woman who had lost her daughter and the hopes and dreams that went along with that. "You have a beautiful home, Señora Rodriguez, and a beautiful estancia. The views are amazing."

"I *am* sorry we were not here for your arrival, Sophia."

Sophia smiled. "Don't worry. Tomas looked after me. He's a fine cook. Did he learn that from you?"

She caught Tomas's gaze briefly and saw approval there. He should not have worried. His secrets were safe with her. And Maria was charming.

"Nothing beats Madre Maria's cooking," Tomas replied, and Carlos nodded.

Maria patted Tomas's arm and then impulsively went up on tiptoe to kiss his cheek. "In case you haven't noticed, Tomas is family." Maria patted Sophia's arm like she had Tomas's and Sophia bit down on her lip, a little overwhelmed and startled at the immediate intimacy of the welcome.

"We treat all our guests as family," Tomas corrected firmly, but Maria glanced between them, unfooled.

"Aha, aha," she replied, nodding, but her sharp eyes seemed to take in everything. "We will see, Tomas. Now come and eat. We brought dinner from the cantina Carlos likes. It has been a long day. Tomorrow will be time enough for *asado*."

During the course of the meal Sophia listened to Maria and Carlos talking with Tomas. It was clear to Sophia that there was much affection between them all. Often they spoke in English in deference to her, but now and again they slipped into their native Spanish, and even though Sophia couldn't make out the words, she could understand the teasing going on through the affectionate tones and smiles. She didn't have to understand the language to know that he was closer to Carlos and Maria than she had ever been with Antoine's family, or even her own. Affection in her house had seemed to hinge on conditions: scholastic achievements, involvement in the right things and with the right people. Margaret had wanted the best for her daughter, but the one thing missing was what Sophia saw now in the faces of Carlos and Maria. It was acceptance, and it was lovely—even if it did leave her feeling a little bereft.

Many things had become clear on this trip, and the one thing Sophia promised herself was that she would respect and accept herself. She didn't always have to seek approval from others to have value. She glanced at Tomas, who was laughing at something Maria said about Miguel. She didn't need Tomas's approval, either. There was a difference however, she realized, between needing and wanting.

Carlos sat back and listened to the exchange, and when Maria slipped into rapid Spanish once more and shook a finger at Tomas, Carlos looked at Sophia and smiled. Something warm spread through her, a feeling of welcome. After a particularly loud burst of laughter, Maria looked over at Sophia. "I'm sorry," she said, still chuckling. "We forget and have put you at a disadvantage, Sophia, by speaking in Spanish."

"Which is a blessing, as I am sure Sophia is not interested in your stories of my bad behaviour, Madre Maria." Tomas sent Maria a most severe look, but Sophia could see the good-natured devilment twinkling there.

"On the contrary," Sophia countered. "I think they would be highly entertaining. I didn't know you had it in you to misbehave."

Carlos laughed then, the rusty sound so unexpected that they all burst out laughing again.

"Another time, Sophia. When Tomas isn't here to add his *centavos*. My children turned my hair gray."

Sophia laughed, since Maria's hair was jet-black without a streak of the offending colour. "I look forward to it," she replied.

After the meal Sophia offered to help clean up, but Maria brushed her away. "You go," she said, waving her away with a hand. "Tomas said you have kept busy. He has done a good job, our Tomas." Maria spoke of him as though he was her own. How blessed Tomas was to have two sets of parents.

"He must have told you about the fire," she continued, her face falling and Sophia finally saw a hint of middle-age wrinkles around the woman's eyes. "And now so much is repaired. The shop and the pool...he told us you helped with the painting, Sophia. That was very generous of you."

Tomas hadn't told Maria that he'd practically forced her into helping that first day, but his secret was safe with Sophia. She remembered what he'd said about Maria being affected by the blaze, and she was doubly glad she had helped. "It was no trouble at all," she replied. "I've enjoyed my time here, Señora Rodriguez. All of it."

She swallowed against a lump of emotion. She had, even the arguing with Tomas. She'd felt more alive here in a handful of days than she ever had before.

"You call me Maria like everyone else." Maria smiled at Sophia. "And get some rest. No rounding up cattle for you tomorrow. Carlos is here now. I am looking forward to getting to know you and treating you to a real *asado*. We will work together. Do you like cooking, Sophia?"

"Yes," Sophia answered. "Yes, I do."

Sophia bade Maria and Carlos goodnight, but after a pause went to say goodnight to Tomas, too. He was standing at a window, looking over the pampas and the big, gnarled tree standing guard on the plain.

When she'd first arrived, she had felt a kinship with the

tree—it too seemed lonely and out of place. But as she looked at Tomas, and then at the sweeping branches, she wondered if maybe it wasn't more like him. Solitary, standing guard, looking after the Rodriguez family. She didn't know why he felt such responsibility to them, but clearly he did. Sophia felt protected, too, but she also felt sadness for a man who had suffered such a loss that he had withdrawn to the pampas.

"Goodnight, Tomas," she said quietly, looking up at him. His jaw was set, his lips a thin line. He turned his head slightly and looked down at her. For a moment their gazes caught and her breath stalled.

"Goodnight, Sophia," he said quietly, so low that she knew it was meant for her ears only. "Sleep well."

Instantly she was transported back to the previous night and sleeping in his arms. Tonight she would be in her own room. It was the way things needed to be.

But as she walked away from him, she couldn't help being a little bit sorry. It looked like anything that was blossoming between them was over. And despite the extra company and chatter in the house, Sophia went to bed feeling lonelier than ever.

As Carlos and Tomas worked outside, Sophia helped Maria in the house.

The large meal today was *asado*, the Argentine version of barbecue, and Tomas had told her over breakfast that it would be unlike anything she'd ever tasted. Maria explained the different dishes as Sophia finished up her coffee and fresh bread and butter.

Already Maria was bustling about the bright kitchen. Once the estancia started taking bookings again, Maria would be cooking for them, too. But for now it was just the two of them in the quiet, comfortable room.

Carlos would start the grill around noon, and the women would make the accompanying dishes. Dessert, Maria explained, was a particular favourite of Tomas's, cookies called *alfajores*. When Sophia asked if she could help, Maria said she would show her how to make them.

Sophia imagined taking the sweets to Tomas later, a way to thank him for all he'd done for her so far—and one that would perhaps go over better than yesterday's painting. She wanted to see the look on his face when he realized she had baked them. She knew she could cook—at least that was one thing she'd accomplished just fine in her old life. Other than the pancakes yesterday, Tomas had done most of the cooking. But the *asado* seemed to be a group affair, and Sophia was determined to have fun.

Maria put milk to heat on the stove while Sophia washed up the breakfast dishes. "These days it is faster to buy *dulce de leche* in the store," Maria explained. "But I like to make my own." She showed Sophia how to whisk in sugar and vanilla and baking soda. "Then I simply let it cook for a few hours."

"It's that simple?" Sophia had eaten the caramel treat from a jar in Canada. She'd had no idea that it took so few ingredients.

"*Dulce de leche* takes time, but the *alfajores* will take more effort," Maria smiled. "Tomas always told Rosa that he would only marry her if she came with my *alfajores* recipe."

The light went out of her face for a moment, and then she brightened again. "I still try to make them on special occasions."

Sophia averted her head, making a show of drying dishes. "Rosa was your daughter, Tomas said."

Maria's youthful face looked weary and Sophia held her breath, waiting. "*Si*, Rosa was our daughter." Maria's hand paused on a cupboard door, but then she opened it and took out a container of flour. "She and Tomas…they were going to be married."

Sophia made herself move, retrieving butter from the fridge

for the cookies, trying to keep things conversational while inside everything seemed to be churning. The picture on the wall seemed to stare at her. "Is that your daughter? The photo of the girl on horseback?"

Maria nodded proudly. "Oh, she knew how to sit a *criollo* like she was born in the saddle." She laughed suddenly. "Tomas was a polo player, but she rode circles around him, our Rosa."

Tomas and polo? It felt like a key to the missing gap in Tomas's life. "Tomas played polo? I thought that was a rich man's sport."

Maria handed Sophia a bowl. "Tomas is sort of the rogue Mendoza. He chose here over the family business. Even after our Rosa…" Maria sighed, and made the sign of the cross before wiping beneath an eye. "I apologize. I'm afraid you don't get over losing a child."

"No, Maria, no," Sophia said, going to the woman's side and putting her hand on her arm. "I shouldn't have pried. It's none of my business, truly."

Maria nodded towards the picture on the wall, the one that had stopped Sophia many times during her stay. "She was beautiful, don't you think?"

Sophia's throat closed over and she tried not to gawp at the picture. This was their daughter and the woman Tomas had loved. The kisses, the night spent in Tomas's arms…it all felt wrong. It felt as though she had intruded. And to think she had looked at the image in the photograph and had wanted to be like her. She had wished for the happiness, the confidence in Rosa's face. It gave her an unsettled feeling; she felt like a thief, when all along her intentions had been innocent.

"I would have thought Tomas had told you about his family," Maria said, greatly recovered as she patted Sophia's fingers and moved to measure out butter, sugar and flour.

But Tomas had told her nothing about his former life.

"We didn't talk about that," Sophia replied numbly, trying

to make sense, trying to apply what she'd just learned to the conversations she'd had with Tomas. Reconciling that with the man who had kissed her, who had said he wanted her...

She closed her eyes, remembering the gentle way he'd touched her, the way he'd thought she was afraid. And she had been. She'd been afraid of Tomas from the moment they'd met. Afraid of the intensity of her own reactions and feelings, too.

"Sophia?"

She turned her attention back to Maria and pasted on a smile. "What are *alfajores?*" she asked dumbly, not sure what else to say without giving herself away. And the last thing she wanted was Maria reading more into the situation than there was. If that were possible. What would the woman say if she knew Sophia had spent the night in his room? She was nice enough now, but it had the potential to be incredibly awkward.

Maria handed her a wooden spoon, adjusting to the change of topic smoothly. "Cookies. We will bake them and when everything is cool, sandwich them together with the *dulce de leche.*"

The earlier excitement about making Tomas's favourite treat was slightly bittersweet now. She'd wanted it to be something from her, but now she knew the sweets would come with a reference to Rosa built in. Had Rosa made him these same cookies in the past? She must have, if what Maria had said about them being Tomas's favourite was correct. There were so many questions Sophia longed to ask and she knew she had no right to the answers. Maria spoke and Sophia pulled herself out of her thoughts and started creaming butter and sugar together, the sweet smell now repulsive to her.

"I worry about him," Maria said, going to a cupboard for a baking pan.

"Who?"

"Tomas, of course. We love having him here. We couldn't

run the estancia without him. But he has closed himself away from the world. He needs to find a good Argentine girl to make him a home. Sometimes I wonder if we made a mistake, going into partnership. It ties him here too much."

Sophia struggled to keep beating the batter. She would say no more, at least not to Maria. Partnerships and dead fiancées. Tomas had told her that only he'd gone to university and that he had chosen the estancia instead. But it looked as though there was much more to him than met the eye. To think he'd let her believe he merely worked here. Heat crept into her cheeks as she realized she'd been played. She could probably find out all she needed from Maria. But she wanted to hear it from him.

"I am very sorry about your daughter, Maria."

Maria sniffed, but then lifted her head and smiled. "Thank you, Sophia. She was taken from us so suddenly, so young. But God works in mysterious ways. We gained another son anyway. I couldn't love Tomas more if he were my own." She patted Sophia's hand and then reached for an egg. "I see a difference in him this week. It is good to see him happy."

Sophia's head came up sharply and Maria laughed. "Don't be so surprised. He is more alive. Carlos noticed it, too. When you are in a room together, the air changes."

"But I'm…I mean…" What did Maria think had happened between them? She'd expected disapproval, not encouragement. "I'm going back to Canada in a few days."

"Of course you are," Maria replied, adding flour to the bowl and taking the spoon from Sophia's motionless hand. "But I am glad you came. He has punished himself long enough."

Sophia could only hold out for so long, and this latest revelation pushed her over the edge. "Punish himself? Whatever for?"

But Maria suddenly became quiet, refusing to elaborate. "If you want to know more, you will have to ask Tomas."

"But she was your daughter."

The *alfajores* dough was a smooth ball now and Maria began to roll it out. "No, I think you should ask Tomas. He should be the one to tell you. It will be good for him."

"And if he won't?"

Maria looked at Sophia, her gaze sharp. "I think he will."

Sophia felt a blush climb her cheeks as Maria turned back to the baking. Maria had mentioned how obvious the attraction between the two of them was, but Sophia thought she was seeing what she wanted to see.

"Maria, I can see you want Tomas to be happy. But that can't be with me. I'm only on vacation, and then I'm going back to Canada and my life there."

Maria gestured for the cookie cutter and Sophia handed it to her. "Oh, Sophia. You young people. You plan everything out and how it is supposed to work. Everything on a schedule. You're on *vacation*. Don't worry about it, let it go. There will be time enough for life to ask its price later."

Maria suddenly seemed weary and Sophia wondered if her words had more to do with Rosa and Tomas, maybe even Miguel. It seemed to Sophia that perhaps life had already exacted its price from Maria, and she still met the day smiling.

She stepped up to the counter and took the spoon from Maria. "Okay then." She smiled brightly, determined to dispel the cloud that had suddenly fallen over the kitchen. Perhaps she'd felt sorry for herself before, but her troubles now seemed minor, distant. Right now the only thing that was supposed to matter was butter and sugar and flour. She looked at Maria and forced a smile. "What's next?"

They moved on to the other preparations, but a cloud hung over Sophia. Did she really want to unlock the rest of the mystery that was Tomas? And how on earth could she find the time and place to ask?

* * *

Sophia sighed, feeling lazy and contented in her chair by the fire. She couldn't remember ever being this full. The fire blazed as the remnants of the *asado* lay about. There had been beef, so many different cuts, so mouthwateringly delicious, and potato salad, fresh vegetables and Maria's crusty fresh bread. There had been bottles of the ruby-red Malbec that Tomas had picked up in town during their trip. And just when Sophia was positive she couldn't eat another bite, Maria brought out the platter of *alfajores*.

"I should have known," Tomas said approvingly, and with a boyish smile he reached out and took two. He grinned up at Maria. "*Madre* Maria never fails when it comes to *alfajores*."

Sophia took one, unable to resist, but couldn't bring herself to try it yet. She leaned forward in her chair, toying with the sweet as she waited for Tomas to sample his, hoping they would meet his approval.

"You're an easy mark, Tomas, if you can be won with cookies," Maria teased.

Tomas forced the smile to his lips as he looked up at the woman who had mothered him during his rebellious years and beyond. "The cookies did not bring me here," he explained as he bit into one. He felt Sophia's eyes on him and he winked up at Maria, trying to keep things light, though his heart was suddenly heavy. "But they go a long way toward keeping me here."

Maria grinned back and said something in Spanish, then turned to Sophia. "Tomas is one for flattery, isn't he, Sophia? You have passed the test." She laughed at Tomas and ruffled his hair. "Sophia made the *alfajores,* Tomas."

Tomas ran his fingers through his hair, straightening it after Maria messed it. Sophia had made them? It had been impossible to keep her from his thoughts today, knowing she was indoors working side by side with Maria. Something twisted inside him at the thought.

He smiled stiffly at Sophia. "You made these?"

She nodded proudly. "Maria showed me how."

"They are very good," he admitted as the buttery treat melted on his tongue. Sophia nibbled on her cookie as Maria put the plate on the table. Sophia stole a shy look at him and his body tightened unexpectedly in response. Instead he forced a laugh at something Carlos was saying.

This was crazy. It had only been days. How had she wiggled her way into his life so completely? For heaven's sake, he'd held her in his arms all night and now he was complimenting her cooking while thinking about kissing her again. Her innocence did nothing to deter him, except perhaps make him understand he needed to be cautious.

She was watching him and he took a third cookie from the platter, something, anything to keep his hands busy as he tried very hard not to look back at her. He didn't want Maria or Carlos to see what he knew would show in his eyes. Desire. More than that. Caring. He cared about her now. He licked the *dulce de leche* from the side of the cookie before biting into it. Joining the real world again was a bit painful, but perhaps good. For the first time, he felt as if he could leave his past behind him.

He brushed the crumbs from his lap and stood, stretching. Sophia watched him, and he felt his pulse leap beneath her appraisal. Maybe he was feeling the effects of the generous helpings of Malbec. Maybe things were finally waking that had been slumbering too long. And who safer than Sophia? She was only temporary in his life and they both knew it. She would not expect more of him than he was prepared to give. Right now all he wanted was to be alone with her. He had missed her today. He'd missed it just being the two of them.

But first there was another tradition to uphold. He went

over to her and held out his hand. "Sophia. Maria has made *mate*. You must try it. It's practically our national drink."

Maria was at the table pouring hot water into a gourd. "Oh, Sophia. I have made us some *mate*. Have you tried it yet?"

Sophia shook her head, looking curiously down at the gourd. Tomas watched her, amused at her skeptical expression. He'd seen that look before during the *asado* whenever she'd been offered something new and different. She'd pressed to know what some of the selections were and he'd laughed when she'd politely—but definitively—passed. But the *mate* was safe. "It's tea," he explained. "Nothing sinister, I promise."

She looked up at him and wrinkled her nose. "It doesn't look like tea."

He couldn't help it, he smiled. There it was again, the childish innocence that was so refreshing. "It's an acquired taste," he admitted. "But you should try it."

"Come," Maria called, and led the way over to the campfire where they all sat, looking into the flames, relaxing.

"Sophia, I checked my books today. I thought you would want me to get to the bottom of your reservation."

To her left, Tomas accepted the gourd from Maria and drank of the tea. "Yes, of course! I totally forgot to ask you today."

"It does seem we refunded your...*perdón,* Señor Doucette's money when he cancelled."

Sophia's face flamed. "Oh," she said, suddenly embarrassed as she realized she had spent the week here without paying for it. "I see." She tried a smile but it felt false on her lips. "Well, I'm glad to know. Perhaps we can look after the details in the morning, Maria?"

"Of course. And there is no rush, Sophia. Don't give it another thought."

Tomas drank his tea and Sophia couldn't meet his eyes. She'd been wrong all along, and she remembered how bossy and horrid she'd been to Tomas that first day. She'd been wrong about so many things—the reservation was the least of it.

Then he passed the gourd to Sophia. "You drink it from a straw, see?" He said it quietly. "A *bombilla*."

"*Bombilla*," she repeated, staring down at the straw and feeling foolishly adolescent as she realized his lips had been the last on it. She took the gourd and put her lips on the *bombilla*. She sipped the hot brew, slightly bitter but somehow pleasant.

"Now you pass it back to Carlos. And we pass it around until it is gone."

As the *mate* made the rounds no more was said about her unpaid bill; it was as though it didn't even matter. What was important to the Rodriguezes tonight was being together. She saw it in Carlos and Maria as Carlos reached over and took his wife's hand, and in Tomas, who sipped the *mate* and reached for another cookie. She was beginning to see how many things here centered around family and community. It was a far simpler approach to life than she was accustomed to and she found she preferred it to rounds of air kisses and handshakes.

And it was something she didn't dare get used to. Now that she knew her reservation at Vista del Cielo had been cancelled, she knew she needed to leave. She had started to care about Tomas too much. What was left for her here? Nothing. Nothing but getting more accustomed to Tomas, and to Maria's friendliness and Carlos's quiet ways. Used to more sunrises over the pampas and listening to the birds call goodnight through the open window of her room. More pretending that this was her life when it wasn't. Not even close.

When the *mate* was gone Tomas leaned over, his quiet voice warm in her ear. "Would you like to go for a walk?"

She nodded, shivering both from the cool air on her arms

and from the intimate whisper. "Yes, I think I would. I need to walk off some of this food."

More than that, she needed to tell him she was leaving. She was free to do as she pleased—settle up the bill and do what she wanted for the last few days of her trip. It was time for this charade to end and for her to get back to reality.

Tomas informed Maria and Carlos in Spanish and held out his hand. Sophia took it, more affected than she cared to admit by the feel of his warm, rough palm encompassing hers.

But if he had ideas of kissing in his head again, he was sadly mistaken. No more kissing, no long looks, no arguments that served to fuel the passion between them.

No, tonight would be goodbye, and that would be the end of it.

CHAPTER NINE

THE evening was waning as they ambled down the lane, Tomas's stride slow and relaxed while Sophia felt like a bundle of charged nerves beside him. The air held a late summer chill. For several minutes they walked silently, with the sounds of twilight filling the gap of conversation until Sophia understood where they were headed—the gigantic gnarled and twisted tree in the middle of the field.

It stood, a lone sentinel on the pampas, and Sophia reached out and touched the bark, running her fingers over the odd texture. The leaves made a canopy above their heads, cocooning them in semi-privacy. Tomas stood like a shadow behind her, his steady presence making her stomach tumble over itself.

She had wanted privacy to talk to him, but not like this. Not with the whisper of the leaves shushing around them, the single ombu tree a life raft in the grassy sea of the pampas. She had to be strong. Definitive.

"The ombu tree." She looked up at him, wondering why here, and why now. Did he realize he was making it more difficult for her?

"You said you wanted to see it," he said quietly, his hands on the trunk beside hers. "Did you know, some call it the lighthouse of the pampas."

"Lighthouse? To guide lost travelers?" Sophia laughed a

little at the description, but her attempt at lightness seemed false to her ears. "I guess that works. It was the first thing I noticed when I drove up in the taxi. Big and strong but very solitary."

"Like you, Sophia?"

She nodded, watching her fingers make patterns on the rough surface. She wasn't that strong, but she was getting better. "I suppose, maybe a little. But I think perhaps more like you."

Tomas paused, and Sophia waited for him to say something—anything—significant.

But he said nothing. Nothing about the picture in the house—he could have pointed it out a dozen times. Or he could have told her that he wasn't just involved with the estancia but was a full fledged partner. Why hadn't he wanted her to know?

"And what about you? Is the ombu a lighthouse for you, too?" She thought about all that Maria had told her today, even if Tomas was infuriatingly closed-mouthed. Was the estancia the beacon in his life, signifying home? Safety? Was it better for him than what had waited for him in the family business?

"They have shade for when it gets hot." He deliberately put the focus off himself and back on the tree. "And the trunks are full of water, kind of spongy, see? So they will not burn in a wildfire."

Sophia looked up above her at the veil of leaves. "An angel, then, in the middle of the plains?"

"An angel with bite. The sap is poisonous."

Sophia drew her hand away abruptly and Tomas laughed. "Not that poisonous." He came over and rested against part of the trunk, his feet braced on the gnarled roots as he looked into her face. "Like most things in life, Sophia, the ombu has two sides. The pampas is beautiful, but it is also harsh and unforgiving. It is important to learn to respect both sides."

Like Tomas? Perhaps she could, if he'd bothered to reveal his other side. Why hadn't he trusted her? Surely nothing could be worse than Rosa's death. But then, perhaps he wouldn't have said anything if she hadn't put him on the spot.

She looked over at him, his dark form silhouetted in the darkness, and softened. Maybe she was being too hard on him. He'd known Sophia mere days. Was she expecting too much, wishing he'd confided in her the way she had in him?

"The *mate* has made you especially wise this evening," she noted, genuinely wanting to lighten the mood and not argue anymore. She simply wanted to understand. But the sight of him, shadowed by the tree, his dark eyes gleaming nearly black in the growing night, did funny things to her insides. Things she thought maybe she had never felt before, or even imagined. More than chemistry. When she left Argentina, she would be leaving a piece of herself behind.

"You enjoyed the *asado*."

"I have enjoyed everything about being here." She smiled and took a step closer to him, knowing this was the perfect lead-in. "Maria and Carlos welcomed me. Do you know we spent the whole day together and we never once thought to get to the bottom of my reservation?"

"About that…"

"You were right, Tomas, and I was wrong. I'll fix it in the morning, don't worry."

He opened his mouth as if to say something and then shut it again, his brows pulling together. Sophia bit down on her lip, wondering if he'd had the words *I told you so* on his tongue but had held back.

When she'd first arrived she'd despaired of using her savings for the trip. Now she considered it money well spent. She was going back a different woman. A stronger woman. She couldn't put a price on that.

Sophia inhaled, suddenly nervous but needing to say what

was on her mind. "Maria and I talked about things, Tomas. A lot of things."

Ah, there it was. Even in the shadows she could see the flare of recognition in his eyes. But only for a moment. His face cleared and he smiled politely. "She wanted to make you feel at home. It is her way."

Bullheaded man! He knew what she was getting at, and he still deflected. She lifted her chin. "At home in a way you aren't with your real family?"

Sophia knew she was taking a chance. But hadn't he considered she might hear the details from Maria? When he didn't answer, she took a step forward. "Why couldn't you have told me, Tomas?"

He turned away from her so she couldn't see his face, but she heard the frustration in his voice. "Tell you what, Sophia?"

"Tell me about being part-owner of the estancia. And what happened to Rosa. Maria wouldn't tell me. She said I had to ask you."

"Why? So you could pity me instead of wallowing in your own ruined life?"

But she knew that was not true, and what's more he knew it, too. "That is grossly unfair. I did not wallow. I have never wallowed. Was I hurt? Yes. But I came here to start over, Tomas. You of all people know that. Because I told you. And I did every damn thing you asked. And what did you share with me?"

"Sophia," he said, entreating her.

God, she loved it when he said her name that way. She would never tire of the soft tones of his accent. But the gap between them was wider than she'd ever imagined.

"Don't Sophia me. You told me about Rosa, but that was just skimming the surface. You could have told me the rest. When we were out riding, the night that we…"

She couldn't finish the sentence. Humiliation burned its

way up her cheeks. She had confided in him about her virginity. Now she felt foolish.

She blinked back tears. He'd given her understanding and gentleness. But he hadn't given her himself. Not all of himself. Just enough to appease her questions.

"You should have told me," she whispered.

But Sophia wasn't prepared for the way her heart would crack when he admitted softly, "I know."

"Can you tell me now?"

"I don't want your pity," he said sharply, moving away from the trunk of the ombu but staying beneath the protection of its branches.

"Her picture is on the wall, Tomas. We walked by it many times each day and still nothing. You spoke of Miguel, but never of his sister. Not until that day on the bridge. Maria said something about you blaming yourself. Why?"

"It doesn't matter. I've moved on."

She shook her head. His body was as taut as a wire, a wire that would snap at any moment. "No, you haven't."

He turned on her then, his eyes blazing, his body emanating anger and frustration. "Why couldn't we just enjoy the week, hmm? We both knew you were only here for a short time. So what difference can it possibly make now?"

The answer came to Sophia as clearly as the stars hanging in the black Argentine sky. Because she was falling in love with him. That was the strange feeling she kept having, the one she'd never felt with Antoine or with any man before him. It made no sense, but it didn't need to, did it? It was just there, a complicated, tangled ball of emotions for a most inconvenient man at a most inopportune time. The man who had given her coins to make a wish and had understood that she was afraid to make love for the first time.

"Because you want to move on and you're stuck. You've withdrawn from the world, Tomas, and you can't find your way back." She went to him and put her hand on his arm. It was warm, but hard as a band of steel.

"Maybe I have. Maybe I just decided that this was what I wanted. I am happy here."

"I don't believe you."

Sophia was surprised at her temerity in saying that, even if it was true. She was more convinced than ever that his silence was his way of handling his grief.

"You don't have to believe me."

She couldn't help the smile that sneaked on to her lips, turning them up as she conceded the point. "I guess I don't. Perhaps I realize how much being here has helped me move past a lot of things, Tomas. It isn't just being here that has done it, either. It has been being with you. You challenge me, and force me to see things I'd rather ignore. But it is good. I need you to do that. And I have no idea how to show my gratitude."

"When have I needed gratitude?"

She raised her eyebrow at him.

He nodded. "That's right. Never."

"But you have it just the same. And of all the things you've said to me this week—all the difficult things to hear—it has been your silence that has hurt me most."

"Hurt you?" He turned his head to stare at her. "How could I hurt you?"

"When people care about each other, they share things. They don't keep secrets." She swallowed thickly. "I cared about someone once, and he kept secrets from me. Secrets that ended up hurting me very much. He betrayed my trust, and you knew that. Why would you think I would let you do the same?"

"But Antoine was with another woman."

"And you were…"

She let the end of the sentence hang, unsaid, but both of them knew the last two words were *with Rosa*. What she didn't expect was the way Tomas came forward and gripped her fingers in his. The pressure on her knuckles was nearly painful, until he released one hand and reached up to cup her jaw.

"Not with another woman," he denied. "You need to understand. I loved Rosa, and a person never truly gets over losing someone they love. But I wanted to keep Rosa out of it. I was with *you,* Sophia." He sighed, the sound intimate in the dusky night. "Only with you. No one else."

Hope, she realized, was a treacherous thing. It made her heart lift at his words, and she leaned her cheek into the wide palm of his hand. Had he truly not mentioned Rosa because he didn't want it to interfere with them? It seemed impossible.

And if it were true, then what on earth was she to do now?

"Tell me about polo. Tell me about the Mendoza family business."

He turned his head. "I can't. I can't go back. I won't. I'm sorry."

Resignation filled Sophia like a heavy weight. She had given him ample opportunities. Had flat-out asked him and still he refused, ensuring there was always that barrier between them. Leaving was still best, before she got in any deeper. Before she did something she would regret.

"You must be cold," he murmured. "You should have worn a sweater."

"I'm fine," she whispered. If she admitted she was cold, he would suggest they go back, and she wasn't ready to give up her time alone with him yet. These might be their last private moments together.

"But you are shivering."

She couldn't tell him the reason why. She could admit it to herself, but she could not verbalize it. He would think she was silly. He chafed her arms with his hands, the friction sending delicious warmth down to her fingertips.

"It has been a memorable week," Sophia said, knowing she had to tell him of her plans now, get it over with.

"*Si,*" he replied. "More eventful for some of us than others."

"I seem to create chaos wherever I go." Sophia smiled.

"But I didn't take good care of you. Some things..." he paused, frowned. "Some things never should have happened."

It would hurt her desperately if he meant kissing her, or spending the night together. She couldn't bear for him to say it, so she took his hand in hers. "You didn't ask me to go racing across the pampas with my hair on fire, did you? My fall was hardly your fault."

He looked at her head, lifting his hand and twining a curl around his finger. "But, *querida,*" he said softly, "Your hair *is* on fire. Gorgeous flames, like sunrise."

His hand was threaded into her curls now and her body swayed closer to him. She knew he was trying to distract her, and it ceased to matter.

"I bet you sweet-talk all the *señoritas,*" she whispered, desperately trying to keep herself on an even footing with him and failing beautifully. But she regained her balance quickly. "And the other night you said my hair was like sunset, not sunrise."

She couldn't tell if he was blushing in the dark, but the abashed expression on his face was gratifying enough. This was the Tomas she wanted to remember, the one she wanted to hold in her dreams when she returned to Canada.

"That is a bet you would lose," he responded. "I am not in the habit of sweet-talking, as you call it. Not at all. As you can see."

His other hand sank into her hair. "I don't know what to do about you, Sophia. I can't seem to stay away, but on the other hand this seems pointless."

"There's nothing pointless about feeling this way," she

whispered. "It feels wonderful, Tomas." She blinked slowly, opening her eyes again, almost to make sure he was really there holding her. One last chance before leaving. "Don't stop."

Her arms hung by her sides as her breath caught. The rising moon cast shadows on his face that had her heart knocking about like crazy. Was he going to kiss her?

"What am I going to do with you?" He whispered it, his voice silky and with the gorgeous Spanish lilt.

"I don't know," she replied. "But I wish you'd do it soon, Tomas. *Por favor.*"

He didn't need further invitation. As the breeze fluttered through the ombu leaves, he placed his lips on hers, tasting, savouring. The air came out of Sophia's lungs in a soft, breathy sigh. He tasted like all the best things of the day—the rich Malbec, the caramel sweetness of the *alfajores,* even the tang of the *mate*, all combined with a flavour that was Tomas. Gentle and persuasive, he guided her until her body was pressed against his. He was strong and solid, an unmovable wall next to her softness. And she did feel soft and delicate and feminine next to his strength. She tilted her head and slid her hands up over his chest to rest on his shoulders as she kissed him back.

With a groan, Tomas spanned her ribs with his hands and lifted her as if she weighed nothing. His gaze held her captive as he moved them back and to the side, and then braced himself back against part of the ombu tree. Gravity worked to his favour and her body rested against his, feeling all the ridges and planes of his body. She sank into him, losing herself in the kiss, letting everything from her past stay a continent away.

His hands skimmed down her ribs and desire rushed through her as she pressed against him.

A door slammed up at the house, the dull sound echoing through the stillness and Sophia pushed away. This was why she had to go. Another few days with him and leaving would be even more difficult. This could go nowhere. They both knew it. Now they needed to accept it.

"I'm leaving tomorrow," she announced, her voice clear and abrupt in the soft night.

"Tomorrow?" Tomas reached for her, but she stepped back.

"No, please don't." She held up a hand, knowing if he reached for her again she might change her mind. "I can't go on this way, Tomas. There is nothing holding me here—not even a reservation now. What are we doing exactly? Flirting? Kidding ourselves? I'm going to square up with Maria in the morning and go back to Buenos Aires. I've been thinking and I'd like to see Iguazú before I go home. I can do that if I leave tomorrow."

"Iguazú? But that's hours away."

It was, and she knew it. "There are tours that leave all the time. Or I can rent a car and drive. I can read a map, Tomas."

She realized her attitude was quite a change from the frightened, defensive girl who had arrived at Vista del Cielo and she stood tall. "All I will need is a drive back to the city."

"Sophia, this is silly."

"No, it is not," she replied. She wished he'd stop looking at her that way, his dark eyes soft and his hair rumpled and sexy. He couldn't possibly know how hard it was to say no to him. But what other choice did she have? She didn't belong here. She never had. She had only pretended because it had suited her. They were all wonderful, but this was not home. Home was a place she needed to make for herself.

"I care about you," he said. "It's the first time I've cared for someone in a long time. I know it's a passing thing. You have always been going to leave."

Her heart began to crack just a little, knowing this had to be the inevitable let-down. He was speaking nothing but the truth. He couldn't know how deep her own feelings ran, so why did it actually hurt to hear it?

"But I'm not ready for it to be over."

And just like that, her heart leapt. "You see? You say things like that and I don't know what to do with it. We're from two different worlds, Tomas. On borrowed time."

"So we enjoy it while it lasts."

"I don't have any practice with that. I always plan things out, you see. Weigh the pros and cons."

"And how is that working out for you?"

His voice held a trace of smugness, as if he knew the answer.

She ran her fingers over a large curve of the ombu tree. "It's not." She sighed. "For a long time I sat quietly and didn't rock the boat. It was easier to go along with what people told me was best rather than do what I wanted."

"We all have to live with our choices."

"Then respect mine, please, Tomas." Sophia looked up at him, needing him to understand. "Take me to Buenos Aires tomorrow and let me go."

"Sophia…"

"If you don't, I will ask Carlos. And he will say yes."

Tomas didn't answer her, but they both knew she was right. His shoulders relaxed and he sighed, giving in.

He held out his hand and she took it. He led her to a place where the tree root extended, curved and knotted before disappearing into the ground. It was large enough to sit on, and they did, Sophia putting her arms around her knees for added warmth.

"If you are determined to go…I got you something in San Antonio de Areco." He reached into his pocket. "I have been trying to find the right time to give it to you. Now it seems this will be my only chance."

Sophia's mouth dropped open. A gift? It was totally unexpected. "You did?"

"You were admiring the silver jewelry. I had the shop-keeper wrap this up."

Sophia felt a curl of pleasure, bittersweet as it blended with the inevitable knowledge that this was their last night together. The trip to town seemed like ages ago, not two days. He had thought of her, even then? Before the kiss on the bridge? "You didn't have to do that."

"I wanted to. Please, just accept it as a token of your trip. A memento."

He put the small box into her hand. "Open it," he suggested.

Sophia took the simple white box and removed the cover. She gasped at the beautiful necklace inside. "Oh, Tomas."

"It matches your earrings. The amethyst ones."

She reached inside and carefully lifted the chain so that the pendant swung free. The silver pendant was in the shape of an ombu leaf, an echo of the ones that covered them like a veil. There was a marquise-cut amethyst in the middle. "It is stunning. I don't know what to say."

"Don't say anything. When you are back in Canada, you can wear it and remember your time here."

Her smile trembled as she turned the pendant over in her fingers. And now she would have the necklace to remember. Remember learning to love herself again and remember the precious gift he'd given her, even more precious than Argentine silver. The gift of being herself and knowing it was enough.

The thought was beautiful and sad all at once, because it really was starting to feel like goodbye. She held out the chain. "Will you put it on for me please?"

"Of course."

He put the box back in his pocket and took the fine silver chain from her fingers. She could feel his body close behind her and the coolness of the metal pendant against her collarbone. His hand swept her hair away from her collar and a shiver went through her body as she reveled in the simple touch. When the clasp was fastened, he kept his hand against the nape of her neck.

"Don't go," he murmured, touching his lips to the sensitive skin below her hairline. "Stay until the end of the week."

That she wanted to say yes with every molecule in her body was enough warning. "I can't, Tomas." And she couldn't tell him the reason. The last thing he wanted to hear from her was the *L*-word. He did not love her, and she would only be hurt in the end.

CHAPTER TEN

Sophia had her bags all packed when Tomas entered the kitchen the next morning. He stood in the doorway for a few moments, listening to her talk with Maria and Carlos. He'd meant to be up early, to talk to her about her plans, but instead he'd tossed and turned late into the night, replaying their conversation beneath the ombu and wondering if she was really right after all. Had he simply been hiding? Running? He thought of his family back in Buenos Aires, and of Motores Mendoza. He had closed the door to them and had been determined never to open it again. He'd flatly refused to talk to Sophia about it. And why?

Because it was easier to forget than to face the truth. He'd said goodbye to his old life and started over at Vista del Cielo.

And what had it fixed? Nothing. And then along had come Sophia.

Did she really have any idea of what she'd done?

She was folding something—was that her receipt?—and tucking it into her purse. She was really leaving, then. Sticking to her guns.

He admired her for it, but he couldn't let her go. Not yet.

He pushed off the door frame and came into the kitchen. "Oh, Tomas," Maria said, giving him a good-morning smile. "Sophia just told us of her plans. I'm sure she'll have a wonderful time. Iguazú is so beautiful."

"So you've straightened out the bill?"

Sophia looked up, met his gaze with her own. Firmly, no shyness or evasion. *Dios,* when had she become so strong? He swallowed as his throat felt dry. Today she was back in one of her tidy designer dresses, bronze shoes on her feet that seemed to be constructed of threads—how could something that flimsy hold someone's weight? And yet he couldn't deny how the criss-cross pattern drew his gaze to her ankles and the smooth calves leading to her hemline.

"I've paid Maria for my time here," Sophia explained. "The mix-up is fixed. Thank you—especially you, Tomas, for a lovely stay."

She was far too composed and Tomas felt annoyance build, tensing his shoulders. Lying awake meant he'd slept longer than he'd expected. He'd intended on speaking to her this morning. The idea of her paying for the week didn't sit well with him. He had expected an argument, but he also wanted her to know that he would look after the costs of her stay.

This way made it seem like she was no more than a guest, and she was. Much more.

"So that's it?"

She gave him a cool look. "What else is there?"

And yet she wore the necklace he'd given her around her throat, and the earrings, too. They'd shared things, personal things. It was wrong to have such a cold goodbye, as though none of it mattered.

"I told Miss Hollingsworth I would take her to the city," Carlos said quietly, and Tomas shook his head.

"No," he said firmly. "I will do that." He stood up straight and met Sophia's gaze. "I will do more than that. I will take you to Iguazú."

He was aware of Maria's mouth dropping open and the smile blooming on Carlos's face. And he was aware of the consternation twisting Sophia's features. This was not part of her plan, and he was damned glad to complicate things for her. She'd certainly done enough complicating of her own. She'd waltzed in here and turned his whole life upside-down.

"I don't recall inviting you," she replied. She kept her expression friendly but he heard the vinegar behind the words.

"You didn't. But you'll waste a lot of time going to Buenos Aires, then finding transportation, then sorting out touring the park on your own…it's just easier if I take you."

Every single word he'd said was true. She would face those difficulties, but his reason for going with her had nothing to do with travel time at all.

He refused to let her go. Even if it meant leaving the estancia and driving across country to the waterfalls that attracted hordes of tourists, he'd do it.

Because he was in love with her.

The knowledge seeped into him like rain into dry ground, making everything expand and grow. What a hell of a situation. He did not know what he was going to do about it, but he knew to say goodbye now would be a mistake.

He stood his ground. For long moments their gazes clashed—his determined, hers resisting. He was vastly relieved when she relented, dropping her gaze to her handbag. "All right, fine," she said irritably. "I'm ready when you are."

"Ten minutes," Tomas replied, disappearing back into his room to throw some clothing in a bag.

When he came back out, Maria and Carlos were waiting with Sophia. Maria gave him a hug and her eyes were suspiciously bright. "You come back to us," she said, and Tomas had to pull away. He knew why. Sophia had been right when she'd accused him of hiding out at the estancia. For him to volunteer to leave for even a few days was unusual behaviour. Maria understood him more than most. She knew that taking Sophia there himself was important. And it was more important than any of them knew.

"Don't worry," he murmured, accepting a bag of *alfajores* for the road. "I'm just taking a few days off."

But it was a few days with a woman—something he'd never done before. Not since Rosa, and they all knew it.

Maria hugged Sophia. "You have the recipe, yes?"

Sophia nodded, and Tomas watched a curl droop over Sophia's cheek as she hugged Maria back. "I sure do. Thank you, Maria."

Carlos shook her hand. "You come back any time," he said, his accent thick, but his smile more easy than Maria's had been, not quivering around the edges like hers.

Tomas's stomach clenched. He knew as well as they did that Sophia would not be back.

"We'd better get going," he stated, moving past the group to load the bags in his truck. "It's a long drive."

They were halfway down the dusty lane when Sophia spoke up.

"You do not have to go with me. Just drop me in the city and I will be fine."

"You don't want me to come?" He kept his eyes on the road, knowing if he looked at her now he might just pull over and kiss that stubborn set of her mouth until it was pliable beneath his.

"I…"

"You what?"

She huffed out a gigantic breath of air. "I didn't want to have to say goodbye twice, all right?"

"Maybe I am not ready for you to leave," he said, turning on to the main road in a cloud of dust.

"But I *am* leaving, Tomas. We both know it."

"Not yet," he replied. "I know what you said last night, but not yet, okay?" He reached over and turned on the stereo. "Let me show you Iguazú." And what else, he wondered. What more did he want? It was all impossible. They were from two very different worlds. If he had to content himself with forty-eight more hours, then that was what he'd do.

He would simply keep his feelings to himself. She never needed to know. Sophia had been so angry with him last night, and as much as he would not admit it, he knew she had a right. He hadn't been totally honest with her. She would never love him, he was sure of it. He'd worked too hard at making himself unloveable.

So he would love her, for the last moments they had left together.

Sophia finished the last of her coffee and put the empty paper cup in the cup holder as Tomas pulled into the parking lot at the Iguazú National Park and killed the ignition. "This is the best time to get started, before all the tour groups come in," Tomas said, sliding out of the driver's side and hefting a day pack on his shoulder. "Later this morning it'll be packed."

Sophia hopped out, clad in jeans and sneakers and a cotton T-shirt. The air was heavier here, rich with moisture and the scent of the rain forest. She followed Tomas to the entrance of the pathways and wondered if it were possible to absorb each detail, cataloguing each sight and scent and sound into her brain so she could recall it perfectly later.

They hadn't arrived in Puerto Iguazú until after dinner last night and Tomas had booked them into a hotel. She'd expected awkwardness, but he'd assumed she wanted separate rooms and had booked them next to each other. He'd handed her the keycard and she had tucked it into her pocket, reaching for her carry-on to avoid looking into his face. She would have insisted on her own room anyway, but it still stung that there hadn't even been a hint of indecision in his eyes. He'd helped her with her bags and without so much as a peck on the cheek or a squeeze of her hand he'd left her to freshen up.

Over dinner he'd given her a little history of the area and

this morning he'd pulled out a park map and they'd planned their day while grabbing a quick breakfast.

Absolutely nothing personal. No talking about Rosa, or his family, or the hour of her departure that was racing towards her faster than she wanted to admit. No words about their kisses or anything remotely intimate.

It was driving her absolutely, completely crazy.

She grabbed his arm as they walked down the pathway, sidestepping to avoid a group of German tourists who, like them, were getting an early start.

"Tomas, please," she whispered, her fingers digging into his arm.

He stopped, looked down at her. Waited.

She had to swallow back the hitch in her breath as she gazed up at him. When had he become everything? Why did this have to happen now, a world away? Even if she did admit her feelings, what good would it do? His life was here. Her family—her life—was in Ottawa. Worlds apart. Tomorrow she'd say goodbye to him forever. The very thought made her feel empty inside, as though a great cavern had opened up, her emotions echoing off the sides. There was no sense fighting her feelings now. The damage was already done.

"What is it?" He reached for her arm, gripping it just below her shoulder, his gaze plumbing hers, searching for answers she didn't have.

"I just can't take this…this impersonal way you are with me. Are you angry with me? Did I do something wrong?"

As soon as the words left her mouth she closed her eyes. She was still afraid, after all the progress she'd made. Tomas had been distant and polite ever since the night under the ombu. Her lip quivered. The very moment she had realized her true feelings, he had locked his away.

"No, *querida*. I am not angry."

"But you…"

He placed a finger over her lips, halting her words, and

then gently touched his mouth to hers, hovering, tasting, their breaths mingling in the humid air of the rain forest.

Tomas felt his heart pound against his ribs as he forced himself to go slowly, gently. Now her lips were parted beneath his and he drank in her flavour, soft and sweet and tasting like strawberry lip gloss.

Reluctantly he pulled away, but he couldn't shift his gaze away from her face. Her dark eyes were dreamy, the pupils dilated and her lips were full and puffy.

"Tomas…" She murmured his name and he watched, mesmerized, as a bright yellow butterfly paused and perched on a burnished curl of her hair.

"Wait," he whispered, releasing her. He let the backpack slide from his shoulder and reached in to take out a small camera. "Smile," he commanded, and he was instantly gratified as her lips curved in a slow, sexy smile.

He snapped the photo and looked at it in the viewfinder, struck by the vivid colours. Her auburn hair, the bloom in her cheeks from being freshly kissed, the depths of her eyes that made her look as if she was sharing a secret with the camera, the shocking yellow hue of the butterfly and the vibrant green of the jungle forming the backdrop. This was how he wanted to remember her—still soft and flushed after his kisses. Full of colour and light and life. The person who had brought such colour back to his own life.

"Come on," he said, uncomfortable at the strength of his reaction to a simple snapshot. Sophia shook her curls and the butterfly flitted off. "We have to catch the train, or we'll miss it and have to wait another half hour."

They caught the train that took them to the *Garganta del Diablo*—the Devil's Throat. Tomas had made this trip before, and knew what to expect, but he loved watching Sophia's face as they went deeper through the rain forest toward the most famous part of the falls. Her eyes danced and she twisted in her seat, looking out of the open window and trying to see everything. His kiss had stopped her questions, but for how long? What if she knew the whole truth? Would she feel the same? Or would that light in her eyes dim just a bit knowing he wasn't the man she thought he was?

Tomas would not let it ruin their day. He pointed out birds as they went along, and cautioned Sophia to put on her poncho unless she favoured getting wet. "The day is clear, but the mist never goes away," he explained. "And Sophia—you will get wet," he promised, as they followed the rest of the throng to the boardwalk.

The roar of the water was deafening as their shoes clunked along the metal structure. They hadn't gone far when Sophia clutched at his hand, her eyes huge as she looked up at him. "The water is moving so fast." The shore was behind them and a thick cloud of mist indicated their destination—the cusp of the Devil's Throat. Right now the only thing standing between them and the rushing water was a metal grate.

"It's safe," Tomas assured her, keeping her hand in his. "And the view is so worth it. Come on, Sophia." He pulled her along, keeping her close as he sensed her unease. The vibration of the water shimmered up through the soles of their shoes. It was impossible to ignore the river's power.

When they reached the end of the boardwalk, the mist hovered, a filmy cloud settling on their clear ponchos. As they approached the rail, Tomas heard her gasp with pleasure, her hesitation temporarily forgotten. "Tomas, look! A rainbow!"

The sun was shining through the mist and an arc of colour decorated the view. "See the birds?" he called to her above the falls' roar as they tumbled and crashed to an invisible bottom. The birds were dark darts, flitting in and out of view.

"It's incredible."

Tomas took out his camera, wanting to capture her this alive, looking so free and vibrant. Did she know how brave, how gutsy she was to come on this trip alone, to gamely take on anything he suggested? Sometimes even foolishly. She was the kind of woman a man would be proud to call his. A woman who would walk beside her man so they could face things together, given the chance. Her ex had to be the biggest fool on earth to throw that away.

She stood on tiptoe, hanging on to the railing and looking down into the cleft in the rock. As the wind tossed her hair over her shoulder, he knew that she was the kind of woman *he* could easily spend his life with.

The realization was so sudden that he felt everything within him drop to his feet, shifting the grate beneath the soles of his shoes. A lifetime? Impossible. Recognizing his feelings as love was different than contemplating forever. He'd felt that longing with Rosa, and he never wanted to go through that pain again. His brain leapt ahead, searching for logic. What kind of life would they have? He could resume his place at Motores Mendoza, he supposed, but he'd be miserable, stuck in the city with no room to breathe. At the mercy of the boardroom and his father's legacy. And the estancia was a fine place for a holiday, but would a woman like Sophia ever be happy out in the middle of the pampas? Living there wasn't the same as a week's vacation.

He took several steps away from the observation platform, back towards where the boardwalk narrowed. Sophia looked back at him and smiled, her curls darker now from the damp, the corkscrews springing up and framing her tanned face. Even if they could agree, it was crazy to think of asking her to stay after only a week of knowing her. The heavy feeling in his chest, the way his words felt as though they were going to stick in his throat when she was around—this was simply a holiday fling, right? A far cry from building a life with someone. That was complete and utter nonsense.

Sophia was mesmerized by the thunder of the water and the spray that settled like a film on her hair. It was majestic, staggering, awesome. She closed her eyes, listening to the crash of the water, feeling the power vibrate through her feet up her body, loving the way the mist moistened her skin.

And then she opened her eyes and looked at Tomas. He was standing back towards the opening of the observation deck, watching her with such a serious expression that her heart stuttered.

She smiled at him, wanting to see him smile back at her, needing the warmth of it. Every time she thought about leaving she felt a little piece of her heart break away. Tomorrow it was back to Buenos Aires and the airport. It was hours on a plane and a life of uncertainty waiting—a life she could choose. It should have felt like a world of excitement and possibility.

Right now it just felt empty. Because there would be no Tomas in it.

She took her hand off the railing and went to him, curling her hand around his arm. "You're looking glum."

"Am I? I didn't mean to." But there was something in his voice. It was too perfect, too cautious. "Let's walk. There are tons of trails. Let's just enjoy the day, okay?"

They made their way to the train and soon they were chugging their way back to the station where they could connect to walking trails. Tomas pointed out coatis scurrying through the grass, searching for discarded snacks from the tourists. "Tomas?" Sophia watched a coati shoving a piece of bread into its mouth, reminding her of the raccoons back home. "If I ask you now, will you answer? Why didn't you tell me you were part owner of the estancia?"

Tomas dropped his hand and sighed. "Maria has a big mouth."

Sophia couldn't help but laugh. "It's like you hung the stars and the moon for her, Tomas. She just loves you. She's proud of you."

Was it pain that suddenly slashed across his face? If it was, it was gone just as quickly. "I have money, Sophia. My family owns Motores Mendoza—an auto parts company."

"Is it a big company?"

He chuckled, the sound tight, no pleasure in it. "Fairly big. My father's empire. I chose the pampas instead. I invested my money in Vista del Cielo."

"Because of Rosa?"

She saw him swallow. She knew it was a tough topic, but it had bothered her that he'd let her believe he was nothing more than a gaucho, a worker.

"Partly. Because I love it there. And because I wanted to help Maria and Carlos. I am the silent partner. In exchange for capital, I have a job, a place to live."

"No," she replied, shaking her hair to let the breeze dry it. She could feel the humidity turning her curls into tight ringlets. "That is a business transaction. What you have, Tomas, is a family who loves you. What about your other family? Your real father and mother?"

He shook his head. "I haven't spoken to them in some time. I should have taken my place at the head of the company when my father retired. He felt betrayed when I resigned and moved to the estancia."

"But they are your family. If they love you…"

The train rolled into the station and they got off. Sophia peeled off her poncho and shook the remaining moisture off. Tomas rolled it and tucked it within the straps of the pack.

"Sophia, I never meant to mislead you. Not about any of it. I'm just a very private person. Talking about my personal life just doesn't happen."

"That explains me having to drag it out of you, then." She started down the path, hearing his footsteps behind her. "But the result is that your silence can make a person feel very insignificant and meaningless."

"Not meaningless!" He jogged to catch her and grabbed her hand. "Sophia…I know how he made you feel. I never meant to do that. Never. There were times I wanted to tell you, but how would I bring up such a topic?"

"The elephant in the room." Sophia sighed, and their steps slowed as they walked the route to the lower falls.

The jungle seemed to close in, sheltering them in a green canopy of privacy as they traveled. A toucan flew in front of them and perched in a nearby tree. Butterflies dotted the foliage. Sophia was thinking about getting on the plane tomorrow and wondering how she was going to make it through that.

"After what happened to you, aren't you afraid to love again?" Tomas asked. "Doesn't it frighten you?"

Sophia nodded. "Of course. Once you've been burned... you grow cautious."

"Then imagine if the person you'd loved had died. Wouldn't it scare you to think of loving someone that much again? Knowing how it had hurt?"

The thought of leaving Tomas tomorrow was ripping through her insides, but he'd still be alive and well and riding the pampas. To think about a world without Tomas in it...

"Yes," she whispered. "That would make me think twice."

"Then perhaps you understand why I had difficulty opening up to you, Sophia. You frighten me."

She stopped in the path. "Me?"

"You didn't realize I care for you? You didn't trust my feelings were real?"

"I thought the feelings were all on my side."

Tomas put down the pack. "After all that happened? The kiss on the bridge? Telling you about Rosa? The night in my room? Did you think it meant nothing to me?"

"I...I..." She stammered, off balance. "Of course not," she replied, but then had to confess. "I mean, you were wonderful, but I thought you were just...being..." She sighed. "Nice," she finished.

"I see," he said quietly. "You told me things, but you didn't trust me. I understand why my silence upsets you. I do, Sophia, and I'm sorry for that. But have you told me everything about yourself?"

Her silence spoke louder than any words could have.

"You did not trust me, either. And what do we have if we don't have trust?"

Sophia had no words. Was he right? Did he have bigger feelings for her than she realized? And had she passed them off as if they were unimportant? She had trusted him, but had she trusted *in* him? He was talking about faith, a completely different thing, and up until now she hadn't separated the two.

"Tomas…"

"Never mind," he said. "Let's take a boat ride before we go back to the hotel. This is your only chance, right? You might as well make the most of it."

He shouldered the pack once more and led the way down the path.

Sophia had felt many things over the past week, but feeling that she'd let Tomas down was suddenly the worst of them all. And with only hours left, how could she ever make it up to him?

CHAPTER ELEVEN

SOPHIA saw the boat and instantly felt her insides seize. It was really just a Zodiac crammed with people and Sophia had already witnessed the awesome power of the river—how could a Zodiac compete with that? But Tomas was right beside her, and she refused to back out. She could only let her fear dictate for so long and eventually she had to stand up to it. At least this time she had Tomas by her side. She had climbed many mountains this week. This felt like the ultimate test, and she was determined to face it.

She donned the life jacket provided and took her seat next to Tomas.

The tour started with the guide narrating a spiel about the river and falls but Sophia heard nothing other than the rushing water. Tomas pointed out something on the shore, and she dutifully followed the direction of his finger and nodded, but she had no idea what she was supposed to be looking at. Instead, she could only feel everything closing in around her. The side of the boat pressed against her leg and Tomas's body was an immovable wall to her left. The grumble of the motor was nearly drowned out by the crash of the water, and the wall of river and people pushed in on her from both sides until she could hardly breathe.

All around her there were exclamations of excitement and whoops as passengers got in the spirit of the adventure. But as they got closer to the roaring falls, the cloud of mist darkened the sky and Sophia was surrounded by it as the pilot took them closer, closer, closer.

The walls closed in, dark and with no escape.

Sophia began to tremble.

It had been a mistake. It had all been a mistake. She should never have done this. Why had she thought that this was a good idea? Her breaths came in shallow pants as she fought against the panic. She wanted out, *right now*. And there was nowhere to go.

She tried to force deep breaths, to visualize being anywhere else, but all she saw was darkness and all she felt was the claustrophobia of being trapped. Drops of water crawled down her skin and she shuddered, unable to stop the shaking.

Then Tomas was there, saying her name.

His arm went around her shoulder, holding her as close to him as their life jackets would allow while all around them screams of wonder erupted as the boat passed daringly close to the falls. His left hand came across and took hers and she gripped it, a lifeline in the middle of the terror. Tears streamed down her cheeks, mingling with the droplets of river water that soaked them all. Sophia fought for logic. *This is not then. It is not the dark, dingy basement and I am not alone.*

She was with Tomas. The boat turned, heading back toward the docking area and Sophia went limp with relief. It was over. Sunlight reappeared as they drew away from the falls, the warm light of it soaking into the top of her head. Still Tomas kept his arm around her and she kept her fingers within his.

She turned to look up at him. His dark eyes were clouded with concern, his lips unsmiling. She blinked, feeling the tears warm on her lashes as her lower lip quivered. Tomas leaned forward and stopped the trembling with his mouth. The kiss was incredibly tender, and he let his forehead rest against hers for a moment before sitting back.

But he never let go of her hand.

The boat docked and the passengers disembarked. Tomas and Sophia shed their life jackets and Sophia stepped away to the trail. The ground felt as though it was shifting beneath her feet. Without saying a word, Tomas took her hand and they began the hike through the rain forest that would take them back to the parking lot. She followed blindly, one step after the other, going slowly until all the others of their party pulled away and they were left behind.

A side path opened up and Tomas led her down it, until they stood at an outcrop overlooking the falls, the roar now a distant hum. He shed the pack and turned to her, holding out his arms. She went into them, and the numbness that had sustained her through the Zodiac ride and walk fled, making room for the painful pins and needles of recirculation as her feelings came rushing back. She didn't realize she was crying until she heard Tomas say "Shhhh" into her hair, and she took great gulps of air, trying to regain control.

"Sophia, please don't cry." His voice was rough with emotion. "Please, Sophia. You tear me apart when you cry."

He cared about her that much? She closed her eyes, inhaling his scent that was man and water and fresh air and knowing it was a smell she'd always associate with security. She was safe here, in Tomas's arms.

"I'm sorry," she whispered. "I didn't mean to cry."

His hand cupped the back of her head, stroking her hair.

"If I had known about the boat…I never would have suggested it, *querida*. I'm so sorry. Why didn't you say anything?"

She sniffled, and pushed out of his arms just enough that she could look up at him—she didn't want to be out of his embrace completely. "I thought I needed to face it. I wanted to show you I could be brave." Her lip trembled again but she stopped it. "It wasn't the boat, Tomas. It was…"

She took in a great breath and let it out again. "It was the way I've lived my whole life, and I'm so tired of it. I'm tired of being scared. I'm tired of being afraid."

"Afraid of what?" He placed a finger under her chin. "Sophia, I would keep you safe. You must know that. I would do anything to keep you out of harm's way."

Her heart gave a solid thump at the assurance in his voice. "I know, Tomas, I know." She put her hand on the side of his face and looked up into the eyes that seemed to see her so well. "Don't you see? I could only face it because I had you. And because deep down I knew that no matter what I did, you would be there. Because you are Tomas. Because that is what you do."

She thought she saw pain flash through his eyes before he lowered his lashes, but when he lifted them again his gaze was clear. "What is it that frightened you so much? I looked over and your face was white. And you were crying. But Sophia, you never cry. Not when you showed up at the estancia by mistake. Not even when you fell off the horse. Talk to me, Sophia."

She led him to a bench on the side of the viewpoint and they sat down. Sophia kept her leg pressed against his, needing to feel close to him. "I should never have been angry about you keeping secrets. You were right, Tomas. I haven't told you everything, either. I've never talked about this before," she whispered. "But I need to now. I need to because I want to stop feeling this way."

He squeezed her hand, the only encouragement she needed.

"When I was eight, my father and mother separated. My mother had never been really happy, but when Dad was gone she was really bitter. She made a point of sending me to the right schools and she worked long hours to make sure we had a nice house in a good neighbourhood. But she really didn't see me. I never understood how he could have left us like that. But when I asked about seeing my dad she never answered my questions. It all went wrong when he left, and I would go to bed at night just wishing he'd come back."

She took Tomas's hand in hers, ran her fingers over the work-worn fingertips and strong muscles of his wrist. He had reliable hands. She lifted it to her lips and kissed the spot at the base of his thumb before continuing on.

"We were staying at a cottage in Muskoka the next summer. It was beautiful, but I was so lonely. I hadn't seen my dad in months and I didn't know any of the kids there. I didn't want mom to see me cry—she hated when I did—so I hid in the basement. I thought I'd be left alone there to have my cry in private.

"Someone went out and they locked the cellar door before they left. I couldn't get out. I had left the door open a crack for light, but once it was shut, there was nothing but blackness.

"I cried to get out. I banged on the door but no one heard. I heard them calling for me, but then the voices went away." Sophia suppressed a shudder, determined to tell him everything. He needed to understand. Someone needed to understand—she was so tired of being alone. And he had been wrong. She did trust in him.

"I sat in the dark for four hours. Nothing but the sound of my own breathing, and the scratch of insects on the walls. But I lost it completely when the spiders got in my hair. I started crying again, and it was a neighbour who heard me screaming and opened the basement door."

"Oh, Sophia," Tomas said, holding her close. "So the morning you saw the wolf spider…"

"I know it is childish, but I've never gotten over my fear of them. Every time I see one I feel it crawling along my scalp."

He pressed a kiss to her temple and she sighed, sinking into him. "That's not the worst part though, Tomas. My mother was livid. She yelled at me for playing dangerous games, told me how terrible we looked to our hosts now—you have to understand this was a very affluent area with big summer homes. We looked bad. That was her big concern. And then she said…she said…"

Even now it stung. Sophia knew it was a horribly wrong and untruthful thing for her mother to say, and that it had been done in the heat of panic. Margaret had apologized later, but the damage had been done nonetheless. "She said I was so much trouble it was no wonder my father had left."

Tomas said something in Spanish she didn't understand, but his tone was dark and angry.

"Being at Vista del Cielo with you—it showed me that all my life I've been afraid. Scared that if I didn't do what was expected of me, she'd leave, too. She was all I had left. So I went to the right schools and socialized with the right people and did the right job. Antoine was the 'right' sort of man— well positioned, well-liked, with a shining future. And I'd been doing what I was told for so long that I was the perfect wife for him."

"Until you caught him with his mistress." Tomas smiled a little, and Sophia couldn't help it. She found herself smiling back.

"Yes. That was the deal-breaker. That was the beginning of me finding who I was, rather than who everyone else wanted me to be. Looking back, I can see that my mom only wanted security for me. She wanted for me what she didn't have for herself. It's just not what I want."

"And that is why you were so angry that I didn't tell you about the estancia."

"Someone else has been in control of my life for so long, it felt as though you were manipulating me, only letting me see what you wanted to, rather than the real Tomas. And that hurt. Because I was really starting to care for you."

"And I didn't tell you everything because I was starting to care for you, too, and I thought if you knew, it would ruin what time we had together."

"Why would you think that? It's wonderful that you set up the business with them. They adore you. She was your fiancée, Maria and Carlos's daughter. She is a part of you. Knowing about her wouldn't have changed anything, Tomas. It's not like it was your fault."

Tomas let go of her hand, slid down the bench and stared straight ahead. "But it is my fault, Sophia. Rosa died because of me."

Tomas hadn't planned on telling her everything. Especially today, knowing she hadn't truly trusted him. He'd thought they were over. But the boat ride had changed everything. He loved her. There was no question in his mind now. And there could be no more secrets between them, especially now when she had told him the truth.

But oh, it was tearing him apart to say the words.

"I meant what I said earlier, Sophia. I would do anything to protect you. But I didn't protect Rosa. She died because of me. Because of the man I was. I was like Antoine. I was focused on business. We were supposed to have dinner to talk about wedding plans, but I was working late, trying to finish up a final deal before a board meeting the next day. Rosa called to say she would meet me at the restaurant. She walked instead of me picking her up. But she never made it to the restaurant."

He swallowed. Wanted to feel Sophia close to him, but he couldn't bear to look at her face right now. He wasn't the knight in shining armor she seemed to believe him to be. He didn't want to see the disappointment in her eyes. So he folded his hands on his knees and forged forward.

"She was mugged on the way to the restaurant. She must have put up a fight—the Rosa I knew wouldn't have gone along easily. There were scrapes where her engagement ring had been pulled off her finger. The coroner said she hit her head when she fell. By the time she was found and taken to the hospital, it was too late. And it all could have been avoided if I'd picked her up like I'd promised instead of being full of myself and of work."

"Oh, Tomas," Sophia said softly.

"You see?" He jumped to his feet, moved a few steps away. "That's what I didn't want. Pity. I don't deserve pity, Sophia!"

"So you turned your back on the company, on your family, and decided to punish yourself by isolating yourself at the estancia?"

He nodded, knowing he shouldn't be surprised that she understood. This was Sophia. Sophia who seemed to get everything about him.

"Maria and Carlos never blamed me. Being close to them I was close to her. And I could help them. It was more than my duty. I wanted to."

It had been the only way he could think of to help. Maria needed people around, people to mother. There was no more Rosa, Miguel was gone to Córdoba and the grandchildren she yearned for were a distant hope. "I couldn't stand to see the loneliness in Maria's eyes anymore. We built the place together."

"What about your family in Buenos Aires? They must miss you. And the company. Did you resign?"

"My brother took my place. And my father and mother..." He swallowed. Yes, they had their faults but they loved him. He knew that. The Rodriguez family didn't run in the same circles as the Mendozas, but he'd finally admitted to himself that his parents had been good to Rosa. Their concern hadn't been for appearances but for Rosa, and how she would adjust to the kind of life she'd never known.

Finally, finally, he looked at Sophia.

She was sitting on the bench, her jeans dark with water, the wet patches on her shirt with still drying. Any makeup she'd worn had been washed away in the spray and her hair lay in dark, wet curls. She was the most beautiful woman he'd ever seen. And he knew as sure as he was standing here that somehow he couldn't let her go.

"My father told me there is always a place for me at Motores Mendoza. It was me who shut the door."

"And will you open it now?"

Would he? He found himself blinking as he thought of his father's booming laugh and his mother's soft smile. He had tried to stop feeling for so long, but Sophia had changed everything. She had made him feel alive again—with pain but there was also pleasure. Warmth. Hope.

"I still do not think the company is where I will be happy. For me it is still the pampas and the estancia. It is where I belong, Sophia." He realized it was true. He was through with the city and boardrooms and suits and ties. Even if the Vista del Cielo wasn't exactly as he remembered, he knew he wanted the wild freedom of the pampas, the simple evenings by the fire and the sound of the birds at the end of the day. But rejecting the life was different from rejecting the people, and he'd done both for too long. "But I need to mend things with my family. And it is you who has shown me that."

Sophia looked up at him, in awe of the man he was, a man perhaps he did not even see. A man who had carried the heavy load of his burdens and responsibilities and sacrificed his own heart for it.

She stood from the bench, her damp jeans tight and uncomfortable on her legs, but that didn't matter. Not at this moment, with this man. She knew the one thing he needed, because it was the one thing *she'd* needed her whole life long. She went to him, lifted her face to his and said simply, "I love you, Tomas."

For a fleeting second, shock made a blank of his face as he seemed to struggle to understand. So she repeated it, this time in his own language: "*Te amo,* Tomas."

He cupped her head in both hands and kissed her, a kiss full of love and wonder and pain and acceptance all at once. She twined her arms around his neck as his hands slid from her face down to her waist and pulled her close. She melted against him, wanting his kiss, his touch, to go on forever.

But it couldn't, and knowing that added an urgency, a desperation to the way she pressed herself against him. Now she wished she'd made love to him while she'd had the chance. She wished she hadn't been so afraid. It had nothing to do with losing her virginity. It was about wanting to be as close to someone as a person could be. It wasn't about the physical, it was about loving him wholly.

Tomas's hands settled on her hips and pushed her back slightly so that the kiss broke off. She was breathing heavily and Tomas's chest rose and fell with effort, but it was the look in his eyes that undid her. It was yearning. The same yearning she'd been feeling only seconds before. She wasn't afraid of it anymore.

"*Te amo,* Sophia. And I never expected to love anyone ever again."

He took her hand and pressed it to his cheek. "I don't want you to leave. I don't know what the solution is, but I can't bear to lose you. And we have so little time…"

"What are you asking, Tomas?" *Say the words*, she thought desperately. *Say the words so I can say yes.*

"Stay with me."

"At the Vista del Cielo?"

"It is a lot to ask, I know. It doesn't have to be there…"

"But you love it there, Tomas. It is where you belong." She looked into his eyes, feeling love run through every pore. It didn't matter that they'd known each other such a short time. They knew each other better than many did in a lifetime. "It is where I belong, too, if you are there."

"I want you to make your own choice, Sophia. I love you,

and it is not conditional. Nothing you can do or say will make me take it away. I need you to understand that."

She nodded. "And you need to understand that this is me, making my own choice. I believe in you, Tomas. I found myself in your heart." She put her hand on his chest, feeling the solid beat beneath her fingers. "As long as I am there, nothing else matters."

"They will say we're crazy…"

"It doesn't matter what anyone says."

Tomas linked his fingers with hers, and her heart was full when he knelt on one knee before her.

And it overflowed when he bowed his head and pressed his forehead to her hand for just a moment.

But when he looked up, it was with determination and love and hope in his eyes. "Marry me, Sophia. Marry me and I will spend the rest of my days making you happy."

The falls roared, birds called and monkeys chattered in the trees, but Sophia heard nothing but the thunderous beat of her own heart as she flung herself into his arms.

"Yes," she whispered, feeling the world tilt, shift and settle exactly where it was meant to be. "A million times, yes."

CHAPTER TWELVE

THE dancing had already started when Tomas tugged on
Sophia's hand, drawing her into a shadowed corner of the
patio. Beyond them, over the hill, the ombu tree stood guard,
and all around them the air was colored by the sounds of
friends and family, enjoying themselves at the celebration.

"Tomas," Sophia insisted with a laugh, "we're ignoring
our guests." But the protest was weak and in fun; she had
been longing to be alone with him for many long and tedious
minutes.

"I am only trying to sneak a private moment with my wife,"
he persisted, and her resistance melted when he touched his
lips to her neck.

"I can't think when you do that."

"Thinking is not required."

That made her laugh. "You're teasing me."

With a groan, he let her go. "Only half. The other half is
completely serious, *querida*."

The day had been utterly perfect. It had seemed to take
forever to arrive, though. They had spent the week after the
trip to Iguazú in Argentina. First they had gone to Vista del
Cielo to tell Maria and Carlos the news and ask if they could
have the wedding at the estancia. That had been important to
both of them, but Tomas especially felt he needed their blessing. Rosa had been their cherished girl. Without saying the

words, they knew that the estancia had been refurbished in her memory. Maria had wept a little, but in happiness, because she and Sophia wanted the same thing—Tomas's happiness. Sophia had been overwhelmed at their generosity, and after talking it over, they decided they would stay with Maria and Carlos while their own house was being built close to the creek. The guest ranch was about to turn the page to a new chapter and become a real family business.

Then there had been the trip to Ottawa, making arrangements to move or give away Sophia's things and explaining the latest developments to her mother, Margaret. That meeting had been the most difficult, as Sophia had been honest with her mother for the first time. There had been tears and recriminations on both sides, but now things were beginning to heal. In the end Margaret had insisted that if Sophia were happy, that was all that mattered. Sophia had even convinced her mother to attend today.

Tomas had done some fence-mending of his own, reconciling with his parents. Today they'd taken Argentine tradition and given it a twist as Sophia had proceeded up the aisle escorted by Tomas's father and Tomas had walked with Margaret.

Now the revelry was well in hand as a band played in the backyard and a massive *asado* fed the crowd that had come to celebrate.

"It has been the most beautiful day," Sophia murmured. Tomas's hand slid over her shoulder and down her arm, the contact soft and intimate.

"And you were a most beautiful bride," he replied. "Too beautiful to resist, I think."

He moved in for another kiss but the unstoppable Maria came around the corner and spied them cozying up in the shadows.

"Oh no you don't," she said, shaking a finger at them.

"You haven't even danced yet. And there is the cutting of the cake."

"Madre Maria," Tomas began, but Sophia burst out laughing. Even now, Maria was still the boss, and ever would be.

She went forward to Maria and took the older woman's hands. "If I haven't said it yet, thank you for letting me be part of your family."

"You are our daughter now," Maria said, emotion thickening the words. "Nothing could have made me happier, Sophia. All is as it was meant to be."

Unbelievably touched, Sophia leaned forward and kissed Maria's cheek. "Do I need to call you Madre Maria, too, then?" Sophia smiled tenderly at her, understanding yet again why Tomas loved it here so much. It was the people, the family.

"Of course not. You call me Mama."

Miguel came around the corner carrying a bottle of beer. "I thought I'd find you here in a dark corner." He winked at Sophia and grinned at Tomas. "It's time for the wedding couple's first dance. If you don't want to dance with your new wife, I will."

"Not a chance, Miguel."

Miguel laughed and the foursome made their way into the backyard again.

Lights dotted the scene and a fire burned brightly. Sophia and Tomas had insisted that a regular party at the estancia was what they wanted and it was exactly what they got—food and drink flowing freely, laughter and goodwill and fun. Tomas's father was talking to Carlos and Margaret was chatting to a young professor of economics that Miguel had brought as his guest. It was a blend of old and new, tradition and innovation as the music changed. Tomas's smile was wide as he wiggled his eyebrows and swung Sophia into his arms for a tango.

She put her hand on Tomas's shoulder and admired the ring on her finger. Instead of a traditional band, Tomas had

had one fashioned from platinum and amethyst to match the necklace he'd bought her. She wore both the necklace and earrings today, knowing they connected her past to her future.

"My beautiful bride," Tomas said as they stepped to the music, their feet moving in a one…two…one two three rhythm and their bodies so close together a thread couldn't pass between them. Sophia's long skirt made swishing sounds on the short grass. "You are a princess today, Sophia. My beautiful, Argentine princess."

She saw him looking at the tiara sitting atop her curls. "It was my mother's. And Maria lent me her blue petticoat that she wore under her dress when she and Carlos married. Wasn't that sweet?"

"Not as sweet as you," he replied, gazing down at her with such adoration she felt her pulse give a kick.

"How much longer do we have to stay?" she murmured, and Tomas chuckled as he swung her in a turn and she slid her foot seductively up his leg.

"Impatient?"

Their gazes clashed. "No more than you."

His warm gaze darkened with what she knew now was an edge of desire. The thought no longer frightened her. She welcomed it. She tightened her fingers on the fabric of his jacket.

"You have learned the flavor of the tango well," he murmured, his breath warm in her ear.

"I was well-motivated," she returned, smiling saucily at him—the man whom she now called husband. "How *long*, Tomas?"

"Not long," he said, putting his lips up to her ear. "The party will go on long after we disappear."

When the dance ended, Maria herded them to a table holding the wedding cake with several ribbons cascading over its top. One by one the single women pulled on a ribbon, hoping to pick the one with a ring on its end, foretelling that they'd be the next to marry. When the winner happened to be Miguel's colleague, Tomas burst out laughing and Miguel turned a telling shade of gray.

But then they said their goodbyes, and minutes later were heading back to San Antonio de Areco and the room Tomas had booked there.

The lobby was quiet as they checked in and Tomas held her hand as they made their way to their room. Once inside, Sophia felt nerves slide through her stomach as she took in the turned-down bed. This was her wedding night, and she was completely inexperienced. She wanted everything to be perfect and was entirely unsure how to make it happen.

But then she looked up at Tomas, who had taken off his tuxedo jacket and loosened his tie, and nerves gave way to certainty and then anticipation. This was the man she loved, and who loved her. Nothing else mattered, except wanting to belong to him heart, soul and body. It had been so worth the wait.

She reached behind her and pulled the zipper running down the back of her dress. She stepped out of it, clad in Maria's pale-blue petticoat. Tomas came forward and took her dress from her hands, draping it carefully over a chair. Then he came back and gently removed the tiara from her hair, putting it on the small table.

The nerves started jumping again, clamoring, demanding.

"Señora Mendoza," Tomas said softly, taking her hands and holding them out to the side. "My beautiful wife. You do not need tiaras and fancy dresses. You are so beautiful, just as you are."

"Oh, Tomas," she sighed, still loving how he was able to woo her with his honesty. She stepped into his embrace. "We've waited so long," she whispered hoarsely. "Make me your wife."

With one fluid movement he had her in his arms, and he took her to the bed, laying her gently on the coverlet.

"You *are* my wife," he corrected. "And my life. And I'm going to spend the rest of my days proving it."

MARCH 2011
HARDBACK TITLES

ROMANCE

A Stormy Spanish Summer	Penny Jordan
Taming the Last St Claire	Carole Mortimer
Not a Marrying Man	Miranda Lee
The Far Side of Paradise	Robyn Donald
Secrets of the Oasis	Abby Green
The Proud Wife	Kate Walker
The Heir From Nowhere	Trish Morey
One Desert Night	Maggie Cox
Her Not-So-Secret Diary	Anne Oliver
The Wedding Date	Ally Blake
The Baby Swap Miracle	Caroline Anderson
Honeymoon with the Rancher	Donna Alward
Expecting Royal Twins!	Melissa McClone
To Dance with a Prince	Cara Colter
Molly Cooper's Dream Date	Barbara Hannay
If the Red Slipper Fits...	Shirley Jump
The Man with the Locked Away Heart	Melanie Milburne
Socialite...or Nurse in a Million?	Molly Evans

HISTORICAL

More Than a Mistress	Ann Lethbridge
The Return of Lord Conistone	Lucy Ashford
Sir Ashley's Mettlesome Match	Mary Nichols
The Conqueror's Lady	Terri Brisbin

MEDICAL™

Summer Seaside Wedding	Abigail Gordon
Reunited: A Miracle Marriage	Judy Campbell
St Piran's: The Brooding Heart Surgeon	Alison Roberts
Playboy Doctor to Doting Dad	Sue MacKay

MARCH 2011
LARGE PRINT TITLES

ROMANCE

The Dutiful Wife	Penny Jordan
His Christmas Virgin	Carole Mortimer
Public Marriage, Private Secrets	Helen Bianchin
Forbidden or For Bedding?	Julia James
Christmas with her Boss	Marion Lennox
Firefighter's Doorstep Baby	Barbara McMahon
Daddy by Christmas	Patricia Thayer
Christmas Magic on the Mountain	Melissa McClone

HISTORICAL

Reawakening Miss Calverley	Sylvia Andrew
The Unmasking of a Lady	Emily May
Captured by the Warrior	Meriel Fuller
The Accidental Princess	Michelle Willingham

MEDICAL™

Dating the Millionaire Doctor	Marion Lennox
Alessandro and the Cheery Nanny	Amy Andrews
Valentino's Pregnancy Bombshell	Amy Andrews
A Knight for Nurse Hart	Laura Iding
A Nurse to Tame the Playboy	Maggie Kingsley
Village Midwife, Blushing Bride	Gill Sanderson

**APRIL 2011
HARDBACK TITLES**

ROMANCE

Jess's Promise	Lynne Graham
Not For Sale	Sandra Marton
After Their Vows	Michelle Reid
A Spanish Awakening	Kim Lawrence
In Want of a Wife?	Cathy Williams
The Highest Stakes of All	Sara Craven
Marriage Made on Paper	Maisey Yates
Picture of Innocence	Jacqueline Baird
The Man She Loves To Hate	Kelly Hunter
The End of Faking It	Natalie Anderson
In the Australian Billionaire's Arms	Margaret Way
Abby and the Bachelor Cop	Marion Lennox
Misty and the Single Dad	Marion Lennox
Daycare Mum to Wife	Jennie Adams
The Road Not Taken	Jackie Braun
Shipwrecked With Mr Wrong	Nikki Logan
The Honourable Maverick	Alison Roberts
The Unsung Hero	Alison Roberts

HISTORICAL

Secret Life of a Scandalous Debutante	Bronwyn Scott
One Illicit Night	Sophia James
The Governess and the Sheikh	Marguerite Kaye
Pirate's Daughter, Rebel Wife	June Francis

MEDICAL™

Taming Dr Tempest	Meredith Webber
The Doctor and the Debutante	Anne Fraser
St Piran's: The Fireman and Nurse Loveday	Kate Hardy
From Brooding Boss to Adoring Dad	Dianne Drake

0311 Gen Std LP

APRIL 2011
LARGE PRINT TITLES

ROMANCE

Naive Bride, Defiant Wife	Lynne Graham
Nicolo: The Powerful Sicilian	Sandra Marton
Stranded, Seduced...Pregnant	Kim Lawrence
Shock: One-Night Heir	Melanie Milburne
Mistletoe and the Lost Stiletto	Liz Fielding
Angel of Smoky Hollow	Barbara McMahon
Christmas at Candlebark Farm	Michelle Douglas
Rescued by his Christmas Angel	Cara Colter

HISTORICAL

Innocent Courtesan to Adventurer's Bride	Louise Allen
Disgrace and Desire	Sarah Mallory
The Viking's Captive Princess	Michelle Styles
The Gamekeeper's Lady	Ann Lethbridge

MEDICAL™

Bachelor of the Baby Ward	Meredith Webber
Fairytale on the Children's Ward	Meredith Webber
Playboy Under the Mistletoe	Joanna Neil
Officer, Surgeon...Gentleman!	Janice Lynn
Midwife in the Family Way	Fiona McArthur
Their Marriage Miracle	Sue MacKay